WHATEVER WHISPERS

GENNA BLACK

CONTENTS

Proofreading: Amy Perkins
Cover Design: Genna Black
Cover Formatting: Get Covers
Content Warnings: @ireadtoomuch._

To everyone who struggles with mental illness.

Most of the time the only ghosts are the ones in your mind, but that doesn't make them any less terrifying.

I have loved the stars too fondly to be fearful of the night.
—*Sarah Williams*

1

THE END

QUINN

ARS LONGA, *vita brevis.* The words are etched into the stone above the entrance of Cypress University. *Skillfulness takes time and life is short*—a fitting motto for a college full of students eager to crack open the skulls of the criminally insane and dig around inside their amygdalae and prefrontal cortices.

Metaphorically speaking, of course. While it probably *would* be kind of cool to *literally* dig around in someone's head, that's not my major.

I'm a bigger fan of the phrase *in vino veritas,* but to each their own.

My shoes thud against the aged stone tiles, worn from decades of students trekking through the cavernous corridor that leads to the dean's office. I'd wager that I've walked this hall more than others.

I can feel the gazes of my peers heavy against my skin, as unyielding as the stone walls of the ancient university. Some are filled with longing and jealousy, while others are just plain nosy. They all think that my close connection with the dean is some sort of advantageous thing. And to be fair, in a place like this—where secrets are as old as the ivy that clings to the gothic spires—most of the time it really *is* about who you know, so I can't hold it against them for thinking that way.

I've never cared about what other people think of me, and I always roll my eyes at the students who only want to be friends with me for their own gain. People are too easy to read; they don't want me, they want access to The Assembly.

The not-so-secret society is only mentioned in hushed, speculative whispers. There's a constant exchange of knowing glances and cryptic hints, with students spreading false stories about the figures who control the town's deepest mysteries—namely, my father.

Some claim The Assembly engages in strange rituals deep in the forest just beyond the university grounds, their torches flickering like phantoms in the night. Others say they've seen a symbol—a twisted, black sigil—scratched into hidden corners of campus buildings, the library, even the dorms. Most laugh it off as graffiti. A few believe it's a warning.

The rumors get darker. Someone went missing three years ago, just vanished from campus. People still whisper that they crossed the wrong path with The Assembly. No body was found, no suspects, only a cryptic note that led nowhere. Still, no one ever speaks of it openly.

And that's not even the only case of someone disappearing, not to mention the people who have been *found* dead.

Despite the fascination, no one outside of direct ties to

the society truly knows its name or purpose. Those of us who do have direct ties? We'd die rather than reveal the truth—most out of fear and loyalty, but for me, it's mostly shame.

So, the secret society within Cypress remains a ghostly presence, fueling late-night conversations and furtive glances. It exists more as a phantom of collective imagination than a verifiable identity—and a massive pain in my ass.

Regardless of any assumptions about the privileges I may have due to my bloodline, the reality is quite different from those perceptions. I'm not being shown any favoritism here, and this is a table they most definitely do *not* want a seat at. I've spent my entire life trying to distance myself from my father's shadow, yet here I am, constantly dragged back into it.

I don't bother knocking on the dean's office door, just shove the heavy door open and pad across the thick carpet. I reach the chair in front of his desk, purposefully slumping into it. He wants me to care about this meeting—wants me to be nervous, so I intentionally exude an air of not giving a shit. The door shuts with a definite click, the sound bouncing off the walls adding an extra layer of tension to the room. The leather cushion squeaks as I lean against it, enjoying the small victory because I know it irritates him.

Despite hating every second spent in his presence, I have no option but to come when he calls. Ignoring him only gives him more of a reason to find a way to make my life miserable later, a pastime he enjoys immensely.

His face pulls into a deep frown, the lines etched into his weathered skin only deepening, as if the weight of his self-importance has carved them there over the years. His thinning silver hair, meticulously combed back, does little to soften the sternness of his expression. The irritation in his narrowed eyes is more evident than if someone had taken a sharpie and written the words across his forehead.

"You're late." His voice drips with the kind of authority that expects to be obeyed without question.

I make a show of looking at the nonexistent watch on my wrist. "Only by a few minutes."

He releases a line of air through his crooked nose. He permanently looks like someone punched him square in the face and I often feel a pang of envy that it wasn't me who had the honor.

"I don't have time for your bullshit today, Quinn." This is not the Marshall Ivor the rest of the student body sees as their beloved dean. He puts on a show for them.

I don't get the courtesy.

It's all just a mask to hide the true person underneath. He's been carefully constructing this façade for years, even taking on this job as if he actually needs it. It's really not necessary for him to work at all—both of my parents come from wealthy families. But for appearances' sake, he has chosen to work at the local university, serving its students. It's more socially acceptable than leaving room for people to question his wealth, which has been a common trend for all those in The Assembly who came before him.

People speculate regardless, and they're honestly not too far from the truth when those same hushed, speculative whispers include words like *extortion* and *trafficking* and *cyber crimes*.

I readjust in the chair, slumping further into it as I cross one ankle over the other and tilt my head toward the ceiling. "Get to the point, Dad. New semester, fresh hell. What do you want?"

The list of things he's made up over the years to force me to speak to him is longer than my fucking arm, but there is nothing he can say to make me stick around any longer than necessary.

"Your mother isn't well." I snort. No beating around the bush this time, then.

She hasn't been well for some time now. It changes nothing. I don't look at him because I don't care. *From childhood's hour I have not been as others were.*

"If you could just stop by—"

I pop out of my seat, standing to leave before the conversation can go any further.

I have no interest in entertaining whatever garbage he's about to spout about the reconciliation of our broken family.

Whether my mother's organs are failing one by one or all at once, it makes no difference to me. I wouldn't blink twice if she dropped dead in front of me this very second, and that is no one's fault but her own.

I have always thought of death as the ultimate release, *the great equalizer* that brings a poetic finality to all our stories. She should consider herself well and truly lucky that an existence as pathetic as hers even *has* an end, but I'm sure she believes some aberrant BS about this not being the end at all... and if somehow that *is* true, I hope she spends all of eternity in tortured regret for the life she chose to live while she had it.

Same for my douche of a dad.

I'm halfway to the door before he's out of his seat and rounding on me. He grips my shoulder, something he always does—a petty show of dominance—and it pisses me off every single time. I used to think a pat on the shoulder each time we met was his way of showing his affection, but the older I've gotten the more rough he's become.

Not that a shoulder pat is an adequate affection to show a child, but when that's all you've ever known, you take what you can get.

"Don't walk out on me, Quinn. This might be the time you regret it."

I jerk away from him and keep walking.

Just because I share his DNA, he thinks he can push me around and make me do whatever he wants. That's never been the case, and I'm not about to break now.

He forfeited the possibility of a relationship with me *years* ago.

They both did—him by choosing the disgusting company he keeps over his family, and my mother for supporting him in the name of her precious reputation; the type of notoriety that does more harm than good when all is said and done.

The damage they inflicted upon me as a child is far worse than anything they could do to me now, but the farther away from both of them I am, the better.

He's long dangled my trust fund over my head to keep me in line, and while I want it, I've made it this long without his money. I'll finally graduate soon and can legally claim it, cutting ties with him for good. It's so close, I can actually taste the freedom.

There's a small part of me that doesn't care whether or

not I ever see a dime from him if it also means never having to see *him* again.

But I have played his games for this long; I attend the school he wants me to attend. I come when he calls despite the fact I don't always do what he asks once I get there. May as well see it through; it's more money than I'll ever see in academia and I can't say the thought of that is *all* negative.

As my fingers curl around the doorknob, I glance back at him. His jaw is tight, his gaze unflinching.

"We both know there's literally *nothing* you can say that would make me any more inclined to give a fuck." I shove the door open and let it slam shut behind me. The sound echoes through the now-empty hallway, and I don't look back.

MARSHALL

The parking garage across the street from my office is deserted by the time I finally drag myself away from the day's shit. The dim, echoing emptiness mirrors the bitterness gnawing at me after another futile clash with Quinn. Her stubborn refusal to acknowledge her family is infuriating. My wife's time is running out, and though my daughter doesn't know it, so is mine.

All Quinn has to do is endure a few months of family obligations.

But, no.

She brushes off her mother's illness as if it's a trivial inconvenience.

Less than.

She has no desire to reconcile with either of us despite my many efforts to make amends.

Maybe she really does loathe us both as deeply as she claims.

I have a lot of regrets in my life. I don't regret the money I've made or the comfortable life it's given my wife, but I deeply regret the things I did to get that wealth. I regret not being there for my daughter and the choices I made, like just giving her up to live with her aunt when she was a child.

At the time, it seemed like a no-brainer. I wanted everyone, especially The Assembly, to think I didn't care about her. It was my way of keeping her out of their spotlight and away from any potential danger.

Not to mention the fact that my life was a lot easier without a child in the picture, and my secrets were safer when they were kept just out of reach.

I realize I didn't care about her the way a father should. My mind was muddled with drugs for years, clouding my judgment and making me incapable of being the father she needed. I was so focused on protecting her and the secret information I'd collected over the years that I didn't give enough thought to our relationship.

Her mother just went along with whatever I wanted, like the obedient fearful housewife she's always been.

Now, we're both paying for the shit lives we've lived in the form of terminal illness.

Finding out I have pancreatic cancer at fifty-two makes me want to spend whatever time I have left in peace. But The Assembly won't let me do that, and I can't say I deserve anything less.

I know I can't undo the harm I've caused, but I want to make amends in whatever ways I can—*apologize*. If I'm going to die anyway, I might as well try to escape now. If The Assembly decides to kill me, at least it would only shorten my life by a year or so.

I just need to tie up my loose ends, and on the top of that list is getting Quinn to trust me for five seconds. She's deeper in this shit than she realizes, and I need her to understand just how far; how I've been using her as my little secret keeper all these years.

She'll figure it out eventually, but I'd rather she hears it from me rather than when someone is digging it out of her with a fucking knife.

I feel mostly confident that no one knows the extremes I've gone to, the things I have done in order to obtain tangible evidence to hold over the society's head. I knew I would need it if ever I found a reason to step away, and that time has finally come. But, there is an inkling in the back of my mind— I know the lengths they'd go to in order to find the information they now know I have.

Lengths I have gone to myself for other reasons.

My car sits under a dying light in the farthest, darkest corner of the garage. The flickering bulb above casts an eerie, intermittent glow on my vehicle. I unlock it and yank open the back door to toss my briefcase inside, just as the light gives its final flicker and dies. With a sigh, I close the door and reach for the handle on the driver's side, only to be violently yanked off my feet before I can open it. The back of my head hits the concrete with a nauseating smack, leaving me dazed and disoriented.

My mind struggles to make sense of what's happening. Just as I begin to piece it together, kicks and blows rain down on me from every direction. There are too many feet to count, each one adding another wave of pain that blurs the edges of my vision. Panic sets in, sharp and suffocating, as I choke on my own blood, gasping for breath that won't come. I try to raise my arms to defend myself, but they are heavy and useless.

My fate was sealed the second I hinted at my desire to step down; to walk away from the one thing that casts a sick shadow over every part of my life. I should've known better, should've kept my mouth shut. But there's never been anything more inevitable than this moment, and I was ignorant—*stupid*—for hoping otherwise. How could I have thought... How could I...

Everything fades—the pain, the panic—every thought slipping away as darkness closes in. My last thought is Quinn, and how I hope she'll make it out of this intact.

2

A MASSIVE BALL OF FURRY DOOF

QUINN

3 WEEKS LATER...

I FEEL eyes on me nearly every second of every day lately. I do not doubt that my newfound paranoia is nothing more than mere anxiety; my subconscious telling me I should care more about the death of my father.

I should, but I don't.

The regrets he told me I'd have are nonexistent, and I am not sure what that says about me.

Anxiety is funny like that; you've decided you don't care about something very much but the parts of your brain you can't access and your central nervous system team up and give you a big ol' *the fuck you don't* in the form of neurosis and heart palpitations.

Regardless, my days since his murder have been tinged with a lingering sadness that I have no control over, one that most definitely wasn't present just three weeks prior. It's an odd, disconcerting feeling, and it clings to me despite my best efforts to shake it off.

Our relationship was fraught with undercurrents of bitterness and tension on both our parts. He was my father, yes, but I can't seem to summon any genuine grief about his death, aside from the persistent, unaccountable melancholy. Instead, my dominant emotion is one of relief—relief that the college managed to start classes on time despite the brutal beating and subsequent murder of the dean that had taken place on campus.

I need school because I love it, and because it's the last obstacle standing between me and my trust fund. Even though he's dead, his influence lingers—his stipulation that I have to graduate to get the money is still binding. The faster I get through it, the sooner I can put everything about him behind me. Every delay, every tragedy, feels like another barrier between me and the life I'm so close to starting, a life where I can finally have a place of my own for me and Kronk, and maybe even a better car than the clunker I currently drive. So I'm relieved, not just because classes are starting, but because the countdown to my freedom is still ticking.

The grounds don't feel any more haunted than they have always felt despite this new cloud lingering over the usual bustle and energy of early September as everyone tries to move on from the shock of his murder.

Cypress sprawls across Hallow Ridge like a fortress, its vast campus dotted with ancient oak and pine trees that stretch high into the sky.

Hallow Ridge itself is a quaint town, just a few streets

lined with shops and cafes. The real reason Cypress seems to dominate the landscape isn't that it's necessarily *big* compared to other universities, but because the rest of Hallow was built around the college.

Cypress was initially established to serve the children of wealthy families, many of whom had amassed their fortunes through questionable means. This environment created the perfect backdrop for the rise of The Assembly, an influential group that played a significant role in shaping the community's development. As these affluent families settled in the area, it began to transform. Over time, the once barren surroundings evolved into a small but thriving town, bustling with activity and steadily growing around the college.

Every winding road seems to lead to some foreboding peak, and the students who come from larger cities tend to find the dense forests suffocating.

I love being hidden away from the rest of the world by the imposing mountain range that surrounds Hallow.

As I make my way up the winding sidewalk, tall bushes with unruly branches brush against my arms. The building at the top of the hill is isolated and quiet, except for the occasional rustle of leaves. As I approach the front, a small cemetery comes into view, tucked between the tall trees. The gravestones are worn and discolored by time and weather, standing out against the greenery surrounding them.

The college's first president had grand plans for the small liberal arts school, and many of his dreams eventually came true. However, during his lifetime, his hopes were crushed when his daughter was found murdered in her dorm.

Death and decay are apparently the Cypress U mascots.

The lingering mystery of who strangled her with her own necklace and shoved the pendant through her carotid still haunts the campus, especially for those studying in forensic science or criminal justice programs, not to mention the med school students— *because what the fuck?*

Even after 320-some-odd years, the unsolved case is a gnawing fixation for many of the students and faculty. It's been rumored that her death was at the hand of The Assembly; they don't tend to like it when their members attempt to leave.

When you're in, you're in for life—a lesson I can only speculate my father learned the hard way very recently. His arrogant belief that he was untouchable, that the law didn't apply to him, seems to have extended to the very society that made him feel this way. I can only assume his sense of invincibility finally caught up with him. The protection he thought he had—the favor he believed would keep him safe— ultimately came to an end.

The thought flits into my mind—how easily it could have been me. I guess I'm not the only one who has always been well aware of how little I meant to my father. At least this time that fact did me a favor.

How easily history could have repeated itself...

The weight of Ophelia's untimely death can be felt all over campus, but it is most palpable at the cemetery where her memorial stands. The stone face bears a somber expression, casting a long shadow over the surrounding graves.

Most everyone avoids taking the route that winds around this particular rise, which is why it's my favorite path to class and where I walk Kronk every day around noon.

My dog is a big, fuzzy goofball with a sleek black-and-tan coat, though you'd never guess how cute his personality is from the way he carries himself—like he's always on duty, ears up and eyes sharp, looking like he's ready to protect me with his life. But really, he's a softie, always nudging my hand for pets or getting distracted by squirrels.

Kruz says I should make sure he does his business elsewhere before we come here because the last thing I want is for him to shit on someone's grave and anger the spirits, since Hill Place is rumored to be haunted.

I've never felt the shiver down my spine like everyone else says they feel as they near the gates—or any other part of the school—and I don't believe in ghosts. It's just a fat bonus that we rarely run into anyone.

Growing up, the cemetery behind my house was my playground. I spent hours every day weaving through rows of gravestones, tracing my fingers over the weathered dates and whispering to the names engraved on each one. The air was heavy and still just like at Hill Place. To me, it was simply an extension of my backyard, and the one place I could go that seemed to be out of reach of my parents; it was too much of a burden for them to trek outdoors to hunt me down, and my nannies didn't give a single flying fuck as long as I spent my time unseen and unheard. The constant presence of death did not faze me; I was immune to ghost stories and still am.

Maggie doesn't seem to mind either.

She's wrapped snugly against my chest, cozy despite the bite in the air this time of year. The wind tugs at my long dark hair, whipping strands around my face. Kronk pulls at his leash as we make our way down the serpentine path along the edge of the slope.

This is my fourth year at Cypress U, and Maggie is the third baby I've been a nanny to during my time here. I try not to grow attached because each stent has been brief, but it's been extra difficult this time because Maggie is so tiny and so darn cute. She's got these big, curious eyes that seem to take in everything, and her chubby cheeks make her look like a little doll. Her hair's just starting to come in, a soft, wispy blonde, and when she attempts a giggle—this high-pitched, squeaky sound—it's impossible not to smile.

I've previously cared for a wild-as-fuck toddler and an 11-month-old who loved nothing more than pulling hair and yanking at my nose ring.

Maggie is hands down my favorite.

Her parents are both professors consumed by their careers. Despite the recommended six weeks of maternity leave, her mama was back at work in what seemed like an instant. Today, she's four months old. This means I've spent almost three months loving her with every fiber of my being, only for her parents to tell me this morning they're cutting expenses. Grandma is in, and I am out.

Part of me doesn't buy it. I think when I refused the time off they offered when dear old Dad kicked the bucket, they were probably more worried about my mental stability than anything. It's not normal to react in the way I have, but I won't try and fake it or hide how I feel. If they knew what kind of person he'd been, they'd feel the same.

The loss of my job was icing on the cake. I started my day off in a bad mood after having spent most of the night poring over theoretical explanations and offender behavior regarding multiple victim homicides for a case study analysis assignment. I finally submitted my hard work in the wee hours of the morning, only to wake up a few hours later to a super curt email: *This is wrong. Fix it.*

I thought learning about homicide and serial homicide would be *fun*. Studying the minds of those who dance on the edge of life and death reveals the most profound truths about human nature.

However, in-depth examination of empirical research makes my eyes cross, and my professor seems like a downright ass. I haven't even met the man yet, but so far, his assignments have been fucking killer—no pun intended—and he hasn't even deigned to upload the first lecture video, just assigned reading.

Which is fine, just not my preference.

We're nearing the bottom of the hill when Kronk tugs at his leash again, this time harder, jerking me forward with the momentum. My hand flies to grip Maggie's back even though I have her wrapped so securely she isn't going anywhere.

He's definitely spotted a squirrel darting across the lawn. His leash strains against my grip, digging into my palm with each tug. His sheer strength threatens to pull us both off balance and I prepare to let him go and hope for the best or else he will drag me across campus like the rag doll he thinks I am, which would be per usual and all good and fine except for Maggie.

With one arm wrapped around her, I desperately try to unwind the rope. It's wound so tightly around my hand to keep him close to me that I'm not sure I can release it before he pulls us over and drags us to whatever he has his sights set on. I attempt to rein him in, tugging him back toward me as he continues to yank me forward.

It digs harder into my palm. "Kronk. *Pfui!*"

It's cool to teach your dog commands in Czech until you have to yell at them like a psychopath in public. It garners a lot more attention than one would think.

My face burns hot with embarrassment as he pulls me along, ignoring my protests. He's very well trained and typically does as I say, but he can't seem to fight against his baser puppy instincts that tell him to *herd* when a small squeaky animal is trying like hell to run far, far away from him.

We're approaching people eating lunch at the picnic tables outside the student center, which is exactly what I didn't want to happen.

People are staring.

They're staring as he pulls me.

Staring as I yell every swear word I can think of in Czech, and some in English.

And staring as I spin, losing hold of Kronk and tripping backward over the edge of a metal bench, landing flat on my ass.

Onto the lap of the most gorgeous man I've ever seen.

And his sandwich.

There are definitely condiments on my sweatpants now.

I am temporarily rendered speechless; half because I am mortified and half because there is a deep chestnut curl that's fallen haphazardly across the man's forehead. I can't pull my eyes away long enough to gather my thoughts.

So I sit there.

Gaping, mouth dropped open.

On his lap.

Speechless because... *he has nice hair?*

He has a nice chest too. I would know because my hand is on it.

I snatch it away once I realize and cup the back of Maggie's head, still mouth-breathing on this man who is staring back at me with a bemused look on his face.

The soft gurgle of her first-ever *real* laugh pulls me from my stupor. Her joy at my humiliation causes me to huff a small laugh too.

I look down at her smiling up at me from her baby carrier and gather myself before peeling away from the man's lap.

"Let me help," his deep voice skates across the skin at the base of my throat, his large hand settling just above my hip bone. There is an electric current that starts at his touch, creating a magnetic force I didn't think possible between two people who have not yet spoken two full sentences to one another.

He stands, setting me on my feet when Kronk trots back over with a half-eaten 6-inch sub between his furry jaws. I groan as my eyes dart from person to person in the space around us. I'm not sure who he stole it from, but I'm guessing it was probably the blonde staring daggers at me from across the courtyard.

I turn away from her, my eyes raking over the man's solid torso. You don't see many students all dressed up on a Tuesday morning, but he makes a cable knit sweater look nice. I'm suddenly painfully aware of my baggy sweats and my threadbare Paramore t-shirt, but looking pretty is not a tax I pay to exist in the same space as nice-looking men.

Even if it was, I would still have fresh spit-up dribbling down the front of my clothing and massive amounts of dog hair clinging to my leggings at any given moment.

"Your dog is pretty cute." Kronk swallows the remainder of the sandwich whole and stares up at him. My dog is the picture of innocence as he scratches behind his ear. "But this makes me extra thankful that I am a cat person."

I'm wishing right about now that I was a cat person. Or a gerbil person. Or a snake person. Anything but the person who belongs to this massive ball of furry doof.

Alas.

Kronk knows my anger is short-lived as he plops down next to me, his large body leaning against my leg. His big brown eyes ask forgiveness as he nudges my hand with his snout. Despite my frustration, I can't resist petting him, and a small smile tugs at the corners of my mouth.

"You are such a jerk." He licks leftover mayonnaise from the tip of his nose and I roll my eyes toward the sky. Maggie coos from her place against my chest and I'm momentarily zapped of what little energy I have left.

I plop down on the metal bench and breathe out the longest sigh.

Surprisingly, the man whose lunch I just ruined takes a seat too.

"Sorry about your sandwich," I cringe.

"Eh. I asked for no mustard and guess what they put on it?" He tosses the remnants in the trash bin next to where we're sitting and fixes his eyes on Kronk, who has settled between his legs and is resting his big head on his thigh.

"He doesn't understand the concept of personal space." I pat the side of my leg to draw Kronk away from him, but he side-eyes me like I'm not his literal mother. "He's a good boy. So freaking smart. But he's also stubborn," I say with a laugh. All of those things are understatements.

"He's perfect." He smooths Kronk's fur down the length of his back, his obscenely pillowy lips tilting into the hint of a smile. There's something about him that makes me think he's older than most other students—the subtle laugh lines framing his eyes add an unexpected gentleness to him.

Something warm weaves its way throughout my ribcage, a familiar feeling but not one that's been triggered by very many men. "Yeah. He is."

"How old is he?" A wet spot has formed on his pants from Kronk's slobber, but he doesn't seem to notice.

"Three. I found him under a park bench when he was just a puppy. I wanted to murder whoever abandoned such a small, sweet baby. I probably should have taken him to the shelter since I haven't ever really had a place of my own for him here in my cramped dorm room, but we've made it work. I couldn't let him go when he'd already been cast aside once."

I don't note aloud that I feel a kinship with him for that reason. Abandoned besties.

Kronk is oblivious to my trip down memory lane, still enjoying all the attention he's receiving from his new friend. "I bet you're both glad you decided to keep him."

"I haven't regretted a single moment of it." I smile, and Kronk seems to understand I'm talking about him now because he worms behind my legs and lays beneath me under the bench.

Maggie has drifted off and her hot breath fans across my chest as I brush the fine strands of her hair back with my fingertips.

I feel a set of curious eyes on us. "Your baby seems pretty perfect too."

I smile at him. "She is, but she's not mine."

"Oh." He almost seems disappointed.

I kiss the top of Maggie's head. "I'm her nanny. For now, anyway."

"I see." His lips purse as if he wants to ask something else, but he holds back.

We sit for a beat longer before he checks the time on his phone, then pockets it as he stands. "Gotta get to class."

"You should let me buy your lunch tomorrow." The words spill out before my brain has a chance to catch up. "You know. Because of the sandwich."

His eyebrows furrow and his jaw feathers in hesitation, but it melts away as if he's made a split-second decision. "Sure."

He takes his phone back out and holds it in front of him. I shift in my seat to fish mine from my pocket and tap it against his. Our screens glow as they connect and we swap contact info.

I look down to find that his is just his first name, and his contact photo feels almost inappropriate to have on my device. Not that there's anything wrong with it. It's just that his face is split in a broad grin and he's so attractive it hurts.

I pull my eyes away and flick them to where he's standing. The real thing is even more inappropriate. No man who looks like this should be allowed in public with their sweater sleeves rolled up to their elbows, and veiny forearms on full display for all the world to see.

I force my mouth closed and smile. "See you tomorrow, Jack."

He smirks as if he can read my mind. "Yeah. See you."

3

IS THIS AN INTERVIEW?

QUINN

MY SATURDAYS ARE MAGGIE-FREE, which I am usually happy about. Today it's a rude reminder that all my days will be Maggie-free after next week.

I'm not sure where to go from here. It's not just that I'm out of a job and baby snuggles, I'm also losing a place for Kronk.

I can't say I've ever been upset about not having to rely on my father for anything because he has been absent from my life. However, it's a different story when it comes to financial support. Unlike many others at Cypress who have family to help them out, I don't have that luxury. As a result, I live like your typical broke college student.

For the entirety of my time here, I've lived in the same dorm. The existence of the university's year-round dormitory residency is something I'm eternally grateful for. It's spared me the hassle of moving in and out every academic term, or being forced to go crawling back to a home I'm not welcome in, begging for a place to stay over summer break because traveling to my aunt's is simply not feasible. I think I would rather sleep on a park bench than go anywhere near my parents' home, even now that they aren't there. Kruz has offered for me to stay with her too many times to count, but my setup works and I have never wanted to put her family out.

The dorms are nicer than any apartment I could afford, though super fucking old. They're nothing like a normal dorm, not that I've attended any other college to know for sure, but I can't imagine that many others are so *aged*.

Like the rest of the school, the air in the dormitories is thick and stagnant. *Cold.* Stone walls, stone floors, stone fucking everything, and it's all poorly lit and creepy as shit.

I don't have a roommate because I ended up in the dorm no one else wanted—the one everyone is convinced is haunted by its former resident. Usually, students can't pick their own dorm rooms, but after several people who were assigned this room complained about strange occurrences and requested to switch, I volunteered to take it. I figured that even if it had a spooky reputation, at least I'd have a place to myself.

The only thing scary I've noticed is the black mold growing around the bottom of the walls in the unexplainably *always* damp corners.

That... and yesterday when I felt like someone was watching me in the community showers. But there was no evidence of that, so I chalked it up to my recent anxiety-induced paranoia. *Thanks, Dad.*

I'm overall happy with my living situation, with one

exception: I can't have Kronk here because pets aren't allowed.

I've been lucky that every family I've worked for has been kind enough to allow him a space in their homes. It's an unconventional, complicated accommodation, but one they've each been happy to oblige out of their desperation for hard-to-come-by in-home childcare. He's still with me most of the time because I'm either in their homes with their kids or taking him out for doggie adventures. He mostly just sleeps there, but I'd give almost anything to snuggle up next to him at night too.

If we can make it to the end of the next term, that dream will be a reality. Once graduation comes, I'll be truly free to provide for myself and my furball and start a new chapter away from the shadow of my parents.

There was a time when my parents gave a shit about me before they decided parenting wasn't for them, presumably in the newborn phase of my life being that I spent the first several years after that with various nannies I don't remember —until the day my dad got fucked up on coke and thought it would be a great time to bond with his daughter. A cop pulled him over for erratic driving. I was taken away there on the spot and would have likely been given right back to him if my aunt hadn't stepped in and finally convinced them I would be better off with her. I will never stop being thankful that she chose me when no one else would.

My dad faced no repercussions after that initial slap on the wrist. It's amazing what can be swept under the rug when you're in The Assembly. They don't hold their members to any higher standard in that regard, and even the cops in this town are under their thumb, turning a blind eye to the illicit activities that run rampant. It's commonplace; casually buying, selling, and running expensive drugs. What's low-class when you're poor becomes high-class when you're wealthy, and the Assembly's grip on this town only reinforces that divide. It's just one more reason I loathe every single one of them.

At some point early on, he set up an irrevocable trust I'd receive once I graduated college. I could get it sooner in other ways, but this is the closest life event. Once I've graduated from the undergraduate program, the money will be mine and I won't have to worry about figuring out my living situation going into my Master's years.

He's always held it over my head even though I couldn't have given a shit less. I have never felt obligated to him in the way he wanted me to. It's the least he could have done after leaving it to his sister to provide for me for a large portion of my childhood.

An October breeze greets me as I step outside the doors of my building. The clouds are swollen and dark. They hang low in the sky, casting a duskiness over the campus and blocking out the midday sun. I breathe in the autumn air, closing the heavy wooden door behind me.

I put off texting Jack all yesterday evening. After I finally managed to coax Kronk into his kennel for the night, my mind was solely focused on retreating into the comfort of my cozy little cave after a long, exhausting day.

I probably should have been the one to text first since it was my idea and I am the one who owes him lunch, but I fell asleep before I remembered and woke up this morning with a single text from him: *Emely's at noon.*

I texted back: *Bossy.*

He didn't reply after that.

Even though he didn't answer, I decided to show up anyway. Worst case, I'd have lunch alone and save the cash I would have spent on his.

I walk the tree-lined path down the slope that leads into town. The leaves crunch beneath my feet with each step, releasing the earthy scent of fall.

Emely's is a cute café at the bottom of the incline my dorm is seated atop, and just across the quiet street. The university buildings look so much larger at street level. They tower over everything, often making me feel smaller and more insignificant than I already do without their assistance.

I push open the door and the smell of roasting coffee wraps around me as I step inside. Scanning the room, I don't see Jack yet so I join the line at the counter to order an iced espresso while I wait.

I settle onto a wooden barstool at a corner table, my back pressed against the wall for a clear view of the entrance.

I spend the passing minutes scrolling on my phone and reading over my assignment for the fifty bajillionth time since yesterday, trying to figure out exactly what it is that I need to *fix* since Professor Jackass gave me approximately zero feedback. Just as the barista calls my name, the door opens and Jack walks in. His brown hair is a mess and he looks like he just rolled out of bed before coming, which is highly probable because there's a baby only a few months older than Maggie strapped to his chest. He yawns and a tiny hand reaches up to forcefully shove all five fingers into his open mouth. He jerks back from the sudden intrusion, then his eyes soften as he gently guides the baby's tiny fingers to wrap around his own, planting a gentle kiss on their delicate skin.

Our eyes meet, and a smile forms on his lips, still pressed against the back of the baby's hand.

My stomach does the thing.

I momentarily wonder if he's broke as fuck living off ramen and expired red bull, nannying his way through his bachelor's degree too. It can't be that uncommon of an occurrence. Then I realize we are both whole-ass adults, perfectly capable of having children of our own. Which is scary to me personally because most of the time I feel like a twenty-two-year-old teenager.

I grab my coffee from the counter on my way to greet him. It occurs to me then that this man might be married, and I should not be looking at him like a field scientist lost somewhere in the desert thirsting after a mirage of an oasis.

Even with—maybe even especially with—a baby attached to him and baby vom crusted on his shirt sleeve, I think I am developing a crush.

I take a long drink, attempting to drown all the nerves that have decided to join this party.

I force myself to relax, plastering a warm smile on my face and moon eyes that I aim at the baby. "Who's this little cutie?"

"This is Sienna." His tone is full of affection, and at the sight of me, Sienna twists violently in her carrier, her wispy brown hair catching the light as she reaches for me to rescue her from her confines. Her bright blue eyes sparkle with curiosity, making her look even more adorable.

"Hi, pretty girl." I coo, looking to Jack for permission before I attempt to swipe his child away from him.

"Be my guest," he sighs in relief as he releases the straps holding her in place.

She all but leaps into my waiting arms, clinging to me like a baby koala.

"So friendly, little bear." He caresses the back of her head as she lays it against my shoulder. The gesture feels intimate, not just toward Sienna, but me too because I'm trapped in the middle of them.

It's not as uncomfortable as I feel like it should be.

He gestures for me to hop in line with him so we can order lunch, and I do but I am distracted by the wiggly little girl in my arms. I'm too busy playing peekaboo to notice that he's ordered and paid for *both* our meals until it's too late to protest.

I frown at him while Sienna tries forcing my hand back over my eyes. "Hey. Last I checked this meal was on me."

He closes his wallet and stuffs it into the back pocket of his jeans, which fit him a little too well and I might have just accidentally drooled. "Was it? I forgot."

I give him a look of annoyance. "How do you know I don't have food allergies?"

"Do you?"

Sienna bounces and pats my chest with her tiny hand. She's giddy for no reason at all and it's hard to be upset with such a little ball of energetic joy in my arms. "No. But I might be picky." I'm not.

"Sienna wants you to try her favorite sandwich." We slowly make our way to the table I abandoned to greet them, and Jack pulls up a high chair. I settle into my seat, content to hold her in my lap.

"You can't use the baby against me. She only has two teeth."

"She's working on a third."

I roll my eyes and bounce her on my knees. "Is Daddy impossible?"

She giggles like she understands and is used to his bull-headedness.

I want to address the elephant in the room and can't quite figure out how to casually ask, so I jump off into the deep end. "Are you in a relationship? Married?"

He releases a choked sound of surprise. "*No.*"

"Good because it would be super weird of me to have lunch with two-thirds of your family, neither of which is your wife."

"Sienna is biologically my sister's daughter, but mine in every other way."

I don't know their situation. His sister could be dead for all I know, but my heart still fractures and a long-held bitterness seeps out of the cracks.

The look on my face is enough for him to answer my unspoken question. "She dipped."

How anyone could abandon their child is so far beyond comprehensible to me. I can feel the word vomit creeping up my throat when someone calls Jack's name, signaling that our food is ready. I'm left to gather my composure and when he returns with a plastic food basket in each hand and drinks nestled in the crook of one of his arms, I've stuffed my childhood trauma back where it belongs: away.

I can't say I'm disappointed with Sienna's favorite sandwich. Turkey and apples on a thick slice of crispy sourdough bread with melted white cheddar oozing out the sides—but I'm most excited about the side of pumpkin mac and cheese.

He takes Sienna from my lap to place her in the high chair. She only protests a little and settles quickly when she notices the small bowl of blueberries he's ordered for her. He plucks one from the ceramic dish and smashes it between his thumb and forefinger. She opens her mouth like a baby bird and he places it on her waiting tongue. "What are you studying?"

The abrupt subject change might have given me whiplash if I wasn't so eager for it. "Forensic Psychology. I graduate in the spring. Maybe."

I was being dramatic.

"*Maybe?*"

His quirked eyebrow is far too sexy and I focus on picking at a burnt piece of cheese attached to the crust of my sandwich when I answer. "CRIM 456 might be the bitter end for me. Professor Hollis is such a dick."

He's silent for a beat too long, and when I look up at him he's hyper-focused on putting a straw in Sienna's water cup. "So I've heard."

"At least it's not just me." I sigh and sink back into my seat, relieved. For a second I thought I'd stuck my foot in my mouth, talking shit about his cousin or something.

"Anything I can maybe help with?" he offers. "I've been told I'm a pretty great tutor."

I tap my password into my phone. The assignment is still pulled up, and I slide it across the table to him. "His response to this was simply to *fix it*. No other feedback, no pointing out what I did wrong on an assignment I spent literal hours on."

He reads it over, murmuring the words aloud and mindlessly feeding Sienna as he does. *"The victims in the case were all young women between the ages of eighteen and twenty-five. Targeted because they fit a certain physical profile the offender found attractive. Victims were from various backgrounds and had no apparent connection to each other."*

He refocuses his attention on his baby and offers her another drink before continuing. "Your analysis is too vague. It lacks the depth most professors probably expect from a fourth-year student. 'Young women between eighteen and twenty five' and 'a certain physical profile' are not specific enough for a thorough victimology. You need to detail their socioeconomic backgrounds, routines, and any other potential commonalities beyond just age and physical appearance. Explore some possible psychological reasons why the offender targeted this specific group. Fix those aspects and your *dick professor* will likely be more than pleased with your revised submission."

"Damn. Thanks." I take my phone back and lay it to the side. "Maybe it's just me. I have so much else on my mind. Hopefully I can shake it soon."

He nods thoughtfully.

I wonder how he'd feel if I chose now to drop the bomb of things I have on my mind—including, but not limited to the fact that the police found at least seven variations in the pattern of footprints on my dad's white button-up and bruised into his skin, and me wondering whether or not the long term care facility I've chosen for my mother is the right one.

I guess the nurses and caregivers there can make unbiased decisions about her care with my permission, assessing her needs without the emotional baggage I carry. That has to be good enough, right?

"He could still provide better feedback than 'fix it'," I pout.

"Yeah, he could. Cut him some slack, though. Maybe he has a lot on his plate too." He has a point, but I'm not admitting that out loud. He wipes Sienna's face clean with a napkin while she tries like hell to wrench herself out of his reach.

"How do you juggle classes and caring for a baby full-time?" I can barely juggle classes and caring for someone *else's* baby part-time.

"It's rough." He looks at me pointedly. "My mother helps where she can, but I haven't had any luck finding a nanny."

My heart skips a beat.

"You mentioned yesterday that your current gig is temporary? OW—" He jerks his hand away from Sienna's mouth and inspects the indentations left behind by her teeth. She squeals like she's proud of herself, causing us both to laugh.

"It wasn't supposed to be," I finally answer. "But as of next week, I'm jobless. And Kronk is homeless."

"I thought he was yours?"

"My nannying comes with a stipulation on my part. Kronk can't stay in the dorms."

He swallows a mouthful of mac and cheese. "*Ah*. I see."

My eyes are drawn to how his throat moves when he takes a long drink of water and I mentally slap myself.

He's thoughtful for a moment. "I have a huge fenced yard."

I would be surprised, but there's a lot of old money in Hallow. It's not unheard of for students to already have a nice place of their own. That would likely be the case for me if I had parents who cared enough to actually parent me. "Is this an interview?"

"Do you want it to be?"

I look at Sienna. She cheeses at me with all two of her adorable little baby teeth, the corners of her mouth stained purple. "Yeah. I think I do."

A grin splits his face and my stomach dips again. I can practically feel the pull of his energy, and I wonder what exactly I'm getting myself into.

———

I SPENT the rest of the day revising my paper based on Jack's very helpful feedback. Once I submitted the fixed version it took all of thirty minutes before I received a response from Professor Douche Canoe: *Much improved. Your detailed victimology provides a clearer understanding of the offender's targeting patterns and psychological motivations. This depth of analysis is essential for profiling and investigation. Keep this level of detail in your future assignments.*

Maybe I should give him a nicer nickname.

4

I MIGHT BE LOSING IT

QUINN

IT'S NEARLY pitch black in my room when something wakes me from a dead sleep. The only light is a sliver peeking through the closed window shutter; a faint glow cast by the sidewalk light outside.

I pull myself from my sleepy haze and I feel the weight of someone boring a hole through my flesh with their gaze... which is impossible because I am alone.

I fumble for the lamp on my worn, wooden nightstand and yank the chain. The bulb flickers weakly before dimming to nothing.

The thought enters my mind that maybe the eyes I constantly feel are actually there and not a figment of my overactive imagination; that whoever fucked my dad's shit up might have their sights set on me now.

It would be just like him to drag me into his shit from the grave, though I don't know what reason anyone would have for taking it to that level now that he's not around to feel the hurt of it.

Not that he would have—hurt over the loss of me, that is.

Fumbling in the darkness, my fingers wrap around my phone at the same time the door swings open, causing my heart to come out of my throat.

Kruz flips on the light switch, her long dark curls bouncing around her petite frame. "Why are you already in bed?" She's nonchalant, her big brown eyes sparkling with curiosity, completely unaware that she nearly sent me into cardiac arrest.

I take a shaky breath and close my eyes, focusing on each frayed nerve ending in my body as I will myself to calm the fuck down. "Why do you feel the need to burst into my room without knocking?"

She closes the door and leans against it, crossing her arms over her chest. "What's the point in having a key if I don't use it?"

I eye her incredulously. "You abuse the privilege."

"Whatever." She rolls her eyes and pushes off the door. She walks toward me and plops down on the bed beside me.

"I was napping," I reply, tapping my phone screen to check the time. It's just a little after seven, but I realize I've dozed off longer than I intended. I can't believe I fell asleep and wasted most of the evening. "*Shit.*"

I scramble off the bed as Kruz tucks her legs underneath her, her tight dark curls bouncing with the movement. "Have somewhere to be?"

"Kronk. Wanna come with?" I pull on my boots and grab my flannel from the hook on the wall.

She gives me a look of pure disgust, her nose scrunching

adorably. "I can't believe you walk up that hill for fun. To the cemetery, no less."

"Correction: Kronk thinks it's fun. But it is peaceful up there. A nice reminder of our transient existence."

She rolls her eyes. "Most of us don't want to be reminded of our *transient existence*." She says the words like they're offensive.

"Memento mori, bitch." I flip her off and pull open the door.

She flops onto her back. "I'll be waiting for your return."

"Let me know if Ophelia shows up while I'm gone," I say with a smirk. She's easy to spook and like all good friendships, ours revolves around light mutual bullying.

She pops upright. "Why do you always go there?"

"Because you're an irrational scaredy cat and it's funny."

She scoots to the edge of the bed and slides off. "Well. I'm not staying here now."

"Oh grow up. I'm here alone all the time. It's fine." I don't tell her I'm starting to wonder myself.

Her Converse shoes smack against the stone floor. "Don't care. I just wanted to ask if you'd come with me to a victimology of violent crimes talk in the morning."

"Sure." I pull the door open and gesture for her to exit first. "I could probably use it."

"CRIM still have you down?"

"My brain is a veritable melted pile of goo, but I beat the shit assignment into submission and turned in a less-shit version of it just a few hours ago."

She loops her arm through mine as we walk to the end of

the hall where the staircase is. "Is tomorrow your last day with Maggie?"

"Don't remind me." I haven't updated her on the job situation, so I tell her about Jack and Sienna as we make our way to the bottom floor. "It'll be on a trial basis at first, but I'm hopeful." I leave out the part where his hair is always mussed in a sexy kind of way and the veins that run along his forearms are probably considered public indecency in at least seven different countries.

"Get some cinnamon."

I side-eye her. I'm convinced she has witch lineage. I decide to humor her, per usual. "For *what?*"

"To blow through your door next week. On the first." She is matter of fact, like I'm the one who's strange for not knowing. "For good luck and to channel abundance. You could use it."

She means the situation with my parents, not just because I'm starting a new job in a few weeks. Every day that passes adds another layer of unease; wondering whether today is the day I'll get the call that my mother has passed or something near equally horrendous in regard to answers about my father's murder. I try not to let it show that any of this eats at me, but Kruz can read me.

"Someone needs to blow cinnamon through my limbic system the first of every month." I laugh at my joke, but she's unimpressed.

We say our goodbyes, and I set off down the path that leads into town, heading toward Maggie's house to pick up Kronk. A sudden gust of wind cuts through my clothes and I wrap my arms around myself. The cold bites at my cheeks, causing my eyes to water.

I feel it again—like I'm being watched—and it makes me question if maybe the ghost stories are true. Something scrapes at the surface of my thoughts, a small voice—a whisper that tells me to run.

I am logical above all else, even when my mind betrays me like this, which I can't say has happened often until recently. I look at myself from an outside perspective, analyzing my thoughts and behavior. This is stress, nothing more. And this paranoia comes from my subconscious—the part of me that sneaks up out of nowhere from time to time and feels guilty and anxious that I'm still unwilling to have much of anything to do with my mother even after everything recently.

I remind myself she's not dying because of me. She's dying because she has a buildup of amyloid proteins in her kidneys, and the fact that she is dying does not change our relationship or her past decisions.

Or the fact that she's never shown any remorse.

I shove the unwarranted panic somewhere deep down and keep walking because there's one thing I'm sure of: I don't intend to answer whatever it is that whispers.

5

I'M EITHER REALLY STUPID OR REALLY FUCKING SMART

JACK

I HAD my suspicions that Quinn was who I thought she was the moment I laid eyes on her being all but dragged across the food court by her dog—which was actually pretty adorable if I am being completely honest.

I had briefly hoped that I'd crossed paths with another single parent, but when she divulged the fact that she was Maggie's nanny, that solidified to me that she was the very person whose name has been on everyone's lips for the last month.

Longer, actually.

I'd heard the rumors about her losing her job with the Kaplan family and was honestly pretty surprised to see that she had Maggie with her. That's what threw me off at first.

I *knew* it was a bad idea to engage, to go as far as I did by not only agreeing to have lunch with her but *with* the intention of offering her a job.

Knew, but didn't fucking care.

She's a student. I am a professor.

Nothing good can come of this.

Of course, she's worked for other professors—but I imagine none of them were so viscerally attracted to her in such a scary way.

And the fact that Quinn Ivor comes with baggage these days... *concerning* baggage was something that I couldn't seem to find it within myself to care very much about while I was trying to convince my blood how very bad of a time it was to rush to my cock.

In the middle of the outdoor food court.

In front of the student center.

Surrounded by a huge chunk of both our peers.

I mean it wasn't like a full on erection, nothing weird. Just a little twitch.

Or two.

I thought that once I sat down to have lunch with her, I could bring up the glaring topics for discussion, or at least steer her in the direction of bringing them up herself.

Nope.

I don't remember any part of anything we talked about aside from *let me feed you because apparently I'm a caveman now* and *hey, be my nanny.*

Everything else is white noise in my brain outside of helping her with her assignment. I immediately felt bad for the shitty response I initially gave her, but Sienna had been climbing me like a spider monkey while I graded work and responded to emails that evening.

I spent the other forty-five minutes at the coffeehouse forcing myself to not say any of the things I really wanted to.

Let me drop the kid off at Grammy's real quick and we

can go for a walk. *We could maybe sit too close to one another on a park bench? Talk about forensic assessment and the intricacies of eyewitness testimony? I could take you for drinks after? Go back to my place and strap you to my headboard with my favorite belt?*

And god, *her skin.*

So flawless and taut, it was practically begging me to fuck it up.

I've always had the urge to mark my partners, but the feeling has never been as intense as it is with her. The only person I've ever confided in about this is my best friend, Ezra, who happens to be a psychologist. Naturally, he's tried to analyze what kind of damage might have caused me to feel this way, but I'm not sure there actually *is* any damage.

A person can have non-typical kinks without being fucked in the head.

I don't know what I am right now other than inexplicably *gone* for this woman.

Sienna splashes water in my face from the sink where I'm giving her her nightly bath, pulling me from the thoughts that have been playing on repeat in my mind since yesterday afternoon. At almost nine months old, she's almost too big for sink baths, and I don't like the feeling I get in the pit of my stomach when I think about how much she's grown.

I've gone through the interview process with more potential nannies than I care to discuss, and not a single fucking one of them did I feel comfortable leaving my kid with for any extended amount of time.

I know it's a fat chance that anyone I hire will compare to my mom, but every time I come home from work, I find her more exhausted than the day before. Neither of us want to admit it, but she's a little beyond her prime. While it's fine for her to babysit occasionally, acting as a full time nanny just isn't in the cards for her for much longer.

Sienna squeezes her rubber ducky, squeaking it twice before chucking it at my head and hitting me square between the eyes.

"Oh-kay, bedtime for you, little bear." I drain the water and wrap her up in the towel I sat aside on the counter, and she makes the growly noise that prompted me to give her that nickname in the first place.

She kicks like a little maniac as I carry her up the stairs to her room where I dress her for bed and settle in to rock her to sleep.

Her eyes are growing heavy when my phone buzzes. I take it out of my pocket, expecting it to be another email from a student asking some stupid question that they'd know the answer to if they bothered opening their syllabus. *Maybe I am the dick Quinn thinks I am.*

Instead, it's my friend Stu, which causes me to roll my eyes just as hard.

Stu: Did you ask her out yet?

I haven't admitted to him that I have the hots for my potential new nanny, but somehow he knows anyway.

Jack: No I haven't asked her out.

Jack: And I'm not going to so feel free to give it a rest.

Stu: Can I ask her out, then?

Resounding no.

He's fully aware of how attractive she is since he and the other third of our trio—my best friend Ezra—have both helped me stalk the shit out of her the last few days to make sure she's the safest fit for our girl. Just because she makes my dick hard doesn't mean I would ever blindly trust her or anyone else with Sienna.

Fuck that.

All we found was that she has a pristine background check aside from a few parking tickets. She's nannied for multiple of my former colleagues who all sing her praises, and she's CPR certified. She spends most of her free time either with her dog or in the school library, often with her best friend Kruz.

The only red flag is that she majors in forensic psychology and still has a habit of walking alone at night, particularly through the cemetery, as if she's completely unaware and unafraid of the potential danger in that—especially after all this shit with her dad.

I almost type 'yes' just to get him to leave me the fuck alone, but can't bring myself to do it.

Jack: No.

His next text is an upside down smiley face emoji, and I am not sure what he means by that other than that he wants me to throttle him.

I don't respond, just stand and chuck my phone onto Sienna's changing table as I sway her back and forth until she's fully out.

My heart is full to bursting by the time I place her in her crib, just as it always is when I watch her fall asleep, but when I close her bedroom door behind me a familiar weight settles in my chest, replacing the feeling.

The energy that comes with the beginning of every

semester always makes me restless. I think most people who work in education probably feel the same; being inundated by new students both eager and anxious to get started, way too fucking many meetings that could have—should have—been emails, and the usual political bullshit a person has to wade through when you work at any university, but especially Cypress.

I've been on my usual edge since the end of August—the feelings only intensified as summer break ended, and news of all the terrible shit happening on campus began to spread like wildfire—but I think that of all that, Quinn is what finally pushed me over.

To say that I am unsettled is an understatement. I suspect the only thing that might settle me would be to fuck her out of my system, consume myself with her, and use her body to release some of the pent up stress I feel like I am always dealing with.

I am well aware of how messed up the idea is. The very notion of a college professor harboring feelings for a student crosses so many ethical boundaries that it's almost laughable. Yet, despite my understanding of the power dynamics and the inherent complications, I can't shake the way my heart races whenever she's near.

It's not just the way she looks, though that's certainly part of it. It's how she interacts with Sienna. The warmth she exudes, the way her eyes light up when she's with my daughter—it's overwhelming.

Every glance, every smile she directs my way feels like a dangerous dance on the edge of propriety, and that's with me only having been around her for two very brief meetups.

I am aware that I should keep my distance, that these feelings are probably nothing more than a fleeting infatuation, but the line between professional respect and personal desire becomes increasingly blurred the more I think about her.

Giving in to this desire with the intention to *just get it over with so I can move on* would likely only add fuel to the raging inferno thrashing around in my chest. There is no part of me that would be able to stop myself from carving my name into her flesh so deeply that no one would ever be able to look at her again without knowing that at least once, she'd belonged to me.

Even after I've put Sienna down for the night, showered, and climbed into bed with a book in an attempt to bank the flames, the airflow feeding them doesn't seem to have been restricted by my brief focus elsewhere—they lick at my insides.

Torturously.

I toss my book onto the pillow next to mine, smacking my head against the headboard repetitively when my mind wanders to the image of Quinn sleeping on it instead—her deep chestnut hair cascading over the soft fabric, her relaxed expression as she breathes deep. I groan in frustration, more annoyed at myself than anything else.

Why am I so fucking obsessed with someone I barely know?

Someone probably twelve or more years younger than me, *and* one of my students no less. Not that she seems to be aware of that at this point, which is a whole other issue.

Because she's gorgeous.

And easy to talk to.

And really fucking funny even though she's been through hell recently.

Not to mention she's smitten with your kid.

I am fucked.

If nothing else, *my fist is* because thinking about her now that I'm alone, I've pitched a tent in my flannel pajamas.

My hand curls tightly around my throbbing cock that's straining against my pants. I can feel the heat radiating from my body as arousal floods my senses, making me dizzy and desperate. I give in to the overwhelming urge and yank at the elastic band, freeing myself from the torturous friction of the fabric rubbing against my sensitive skin. I wrap my fingers tightly around my shaft as I try to focus on the physical sensation. For just a few moments, I am lost in the pleasure, begging my own hand for relief from the all-consuming enigma that is Quinn Ivor.

I come hard—violently, hot cum spurting onto my abdomen as I think about all the ways she might let me defile her if I asked nicely enough. I don't even bother cleaning myself up after, because some fucked part of me relishes in the thought that it's the product of the first time I came with her name on my lips.

Eventually, exhaustion takes over and I can find some semblance of rest, but even in sleep, my mind is consumed by her.

6

YOU'VE GOT TO BE FUCKING KIDDING ME

QUINN

KRUZ and I are running late when we meet outside the lecture hall. We push through the double doors, and a wave of warm air and chatter smacks us in the face. It's packed, every seat taken and students are lined up against the walls shoulder to shoulder. We find a space and sit on the cold tile floor, leaning against the back wall, me with my notebook propped on my lap.

"Who takes notes at these things?" She scrapes at her chipped nail polish.

"People who don't know shit about fuck," I say seriously.

She glares at me. "Please. You know everything about everything."

"That's because I take notes," I deadpan.

Taking notes constantly during every class or lecture has always been the key to my success in school. Without them, I struggle to remember anything at all.

I prepare myself for potential impending boredom. I don't know who the speaker is since I'm just tagging along with Kruz, but the answer to that question will make all the difference in regard to how my focus goes, whether it's some old man they've scheduled to drone on for the next three excruciating hours or someone interesting and capable of holding my attention.

And then he steps behind the podium.

His hair is less disheveled today. He's wearing a tweed blazer with elbow patches and thick-rimmed glasses that I haven't seen him wear before are perched on his nose.

"For those of you I am unacquainted with, I'm Professor Hollis. Feel free to call me Jack. I teach Homicide and Serial Homicide here at Cypress."

A loud buzzing fills my ears, and I don't hear anything he says after that. I'm trying to make sense of the fact that not only is he a professor at this university, he's *my* professor. The pieces suddenly click into place and I feel so dumb for mistaking him as a student.

I complained to him *about him.*

I called him a dick to his face.

I want to crawl into a hole and die. Why the fuck did he want to give me a job after that? Maybe he's a masochist as well as a sadist.

How is this happening?

A huge part of me now wonders if he's not actually a dick, but just a dad who is busy with his baby so he gives curt responses. *Fuck my life, I am the asshole here.*

"The majority of you are likely studying either Forensic Psychology or Criminology. Victimology of violent crimes is —" He stumbles over his words when our eyes somehow find one another in a room filled with eleventy hundred people.

I raise an eyebrow at him, twirling my pen between my fingers.

He clears his throat and continues, his gaze flickering to the audience as a whole before returning to me and back again. I can feel the weight of each pair of eyes when half the room turns to look at me.

The curious stares of my classmates prick at my skin, which I should be used to at this point. I am aggressively note-taking—even though Jack has barely gotten past his introduction—in hopes that no one will realize it was me he was distracted by.

I am actually doodling a haunted house, but no one around me can see the page.

Except for Kruz.

She grinds her elbow between my ribs. "What was that all about?"

I swirl the tip of my pen in a circle, filling in the too-big eyes of a small ghost sketch. The ink smudges a bit as I add an evil smirk to his face. He is definitely an old white man politician ghost due to his love of all things malevolent and terrifying.

"*Quinn.*"

I realize I haven't responded. I look at her and widen my eyes, making sure she can see the surprise there. I shift my gaze towards Jack without turning my head, indicating that he is the source of my discomposure and mouth, "*Jack.*"

She stares back at me blankly for a moment before understanding lights her eyes and her mouth drops open a fraction.

Then she punches me in the arm and whispers too loudly, "You left out the part where he's hot as fuck."

"I... didn't notice."

"*Bullshit.*"

I quietly appreciate that my best friend has never once questioned my bi-ness even though I have never had much of an attraction to men. She is an equal opportunity nuisance when it comes to my love life... or lack thereof.

Kruz, on the other hand, jumps from one fling to another like it's a sport, living for the drama and excitement of it all. She thrives on the chaos of her love life, while I've always been more cautious.

I go back to scribbling a roof onto my house. "I didn't want to be weird about it. I'm about to work for him, so there can't be anything between us. Especially not now because he's also apparently my fucking professor."

"This is some taboo romance novel-level stuff." Of course, she would say that.

"There is no romance, Kruz." I am adamant.

She wraps her hand around my forearm and looks at me with an elated gleam in her eyes. "*Yet.*"

I don't argue, because as much as I don't want to admit it, I hope she is right.

7

THE GRAND TOUR

QUINN

THE FOLLOWING week and a half passes in a blur. Each day bleeds into the next, filled with stuffing my mind full of information on psychological profiles that feel hauntingly dissonant against the weight of my father's murder.

I grip the steering wheel as I drive toward the Hollis home, the engine's hum a dull backdrop to my racing thoughts.

Committing to Jack and Sienna is a welcome distraction from the turmoil churning my insides.

As I approach the driveway, I wonder if caring for a new baby—spending my time outside of school work focusing on learning her specific needs—will help me reconcile my own fractured emotions or if it will only deepen the chasm of loss and regret.

My father's yet-to-be-solved murder clings to me, a constant reminder that understanding this kind of darkness on paper is one thing, but facing it in my own life is an entirely different challenge, no matter how much I loathed him.

Jack's house stands tall, dark, and imposing, its wrought-iron gates creaking open to reveal a sprawling yard. There is a long fence that lines the perimeter of the property. It's similar to what he described, but it's not the yard that has my attention—it's the stunning architecture; ornate details, and pointed spires. It fits perfectly with the vibes of the rest of Hollow, but I never would have expected such beauty after Jack's sole mention of having a large fenced yard. I don't know what I expected... maybe a white picket fence? Not this.

Although, maybe I should've thought to adjust my expectations after I learned he is a professor and not a student.

I am a moron.

Drool drips from the tip of Kronk's tongue, adding to the mess of dog hair already covering the front seat of my car. I pull up the driveway and he becomes fidgety and restless, like he knows this is his new digs.

"Fancier than the last place, huh?" I scratch behind his ear as I put the car into park. "So much room for activities."

The front door swings open and Jack steps onto the covered porch, Sienna bouncing in his arms.

I give Kronk a stern look. "Stay put. *Zustan.*"

I crack his window a few inches. He whines as I open my door and step out of the vehicle, but does as he's told.

I thank all the gods that he is showing he does actually listen most of the time. I don't think most people realize how wild as fuck a young German Shepherd can be, regardless of their training. He wasn't exactly impressive during our first meeting with Jack, and I am shocked he even considered offering to let him stay here as an option.

Introducing Kronk to Sienna will be a necessity at some point, but the last thing I need is for him to make a fool of us again today.

"You can let him out," Jack says as I approach the porch.

Sienna spots me and immediately goes nuts trying to wiggle her way free of his hold. I scoop her into my arms, and she giggles with delight. "Daddy is trying to subject you to the big silly dog."

"Da da da da da," she babbles, and I could squeeze her because she's so freaking cute.

"Sienna loves big silly dogs. Don't you, little bear?" He takes her hand between his fingers and gives it a playful shake.

"And I am sure he will love her, but you should know that there is a nonzero chance that he will lovingly freak the eff out. This will all be very new and exciting to him."

"You can say fuck. She doesn't understand what you're saying yet."

"She's what? Nearly eight months old? Nine? She understands a lot more than you th—"

"Fuh fuh fuh fuh fuh." She smacks my cheek and cackles.

I press my lips together to keep from laughing, but a small snort breaks free despite my best efforts.

Jack looks devastated. "It's fine. This is fine. She doesn't know what she's saying. She's not even really saying it. She's too small for words. Oh my god did I just make her second word 'fuck'?"

"Fuh fuh fuh fuh."

I dissolve into quiet laughter.

"This is not funny."

I rein myself in but struggle to keep it at bay. "You're right. It's not."

He glares at me as he opens the door and gestures for me to enter. "It's almost Sienna's nap time. Her nursery is upstairs, the first door on the right. Take her up and I'll release the Kraken."

Release the Kronken. Heh.

I take this as a challenge, fully prepared to show off my super nanny skills. "Good luck, bestie. I hope you're fluent in Czech."

I salute him and head for the stairs, ignoring when he questions what I mean by that. I am most assuredly *not* fluent in Czech; I only know a few commands... and swear words, which we should both probably take up using in front of Sienna now. If she repeats them, at least no one will know what the *kurva* she's saying.

As soon as I step into Sienna's nursery, the dark, moody atmosphere of the rest of the house melts away. The walls are a buttery yellow, cozy and inviting. The wooden crib is painted a creamy white and has intricate carvings of flowers and vines. In the corner, there is an old rocking chair with faded floral cushions that look like they've been loved for years. Everything in the room exudes warmth and comfort.

I don't know if it's part of Sienna's naptime routine, but when I sit and begin to rock, her tiny body wilts against mine and her eyelids droop with the swaying movement.

I brush my index finger between her eyebrows and down the bridge of her nose. I miss Maggie, but snuggling this sweet girl is a balm to the hurt. "You are the sweetest baby." A smile tugs at the corner of her mouth at the sound of my voice even though she's almost out. "I think we are going to get along just fine."

We sit like that for a few more minutes, then I stand and place her in her crib. She doesn't stir, just snoozes away.

I turn to find Jack standing in the doorway. It startles me but I suppress the scream lodged in my throat to keep from waking her.

He smirks at the way I spook. "Get used to being jump scared. I forgot to mention the house is haunted."

I snort as we quietly close her bedroom door behind us. "Yeah, this house and every other part of this town."

"What, you don't believe the stories?" He stops at the top of the staircase and turns to look at me.

"I can't tell if you're being serious." I cross my arms over my chest and his eyes dart to the movement, snagging on my cleavage. I like that my body causes him to falter.

"So serious." It seems as if he has to force himself to turn away.

The stairs creak as we make our way to the bottom floor again. "In that case, I need a raise."

I follow him through the kitchen, the sticky scent of smashed fruit lingering as we pass the table and Sienna's highchair. I am sure I interrupted lunch, and I quietly appreciate that he seems to be more attentive to Sienna's needs than he is worried about immediately cleaning everything up for my sake. Just parent life things, and I am more than understanding.

I'm sure I'll see bigger messes than this one if I stick

around for any length of time, so there's no use in him cleaning up for my sake now.

"We haven't even discussed your pay."

I try not to gape too obviously at stunning wooden cabinets and dark granite countertops, but I'm practically panting at the thought of cooking here. "You're right. This kitchen is payment enough."

"You like to cook?" He opens the door and Kronk gallops toward us from across the massive yard. His feet pounding against the stone back patio sound like a herd of bison.

As a kid, cooking gave me a sense of self-sufficiency I was hard-pressed to find anywhere else. In a household where my parents were accustomed to being waited on hand and foot by hired help, it felt like an act of rebellion to take matters into my own hands and prepare my own meals, as simple as they had to be given my age and the limitations that came with that.

Not to mention that I all but got off on their disapproval of it.

Cooking was not just food to me, it was a means of keeping my body and soul together—the one way I could achieve both independence and defiance for a long time.

"I do. And I'm afraid to say that the miniature microwave I use to make ramen in my dorm is just not the same as having an actual kitchen."

"Ah." I can see the wheels turning in his mind, about what I am unsure of.

Kronk almost bowls me over once he reaches us.

"You like this big fancy yard?" I crouch down and aggressively scratch on either side of his head prompting him to lick the side of my neck. "Gross, you furry beast."

He doubles down on the gross factor and licks my face, placing a paw on my shoulder. The unexpected force of it causes me to lose my balance.

I tip backwards onto my ass and Jack lets out a throaty chuckle. "He's always making you fall, huh?"

He extends his hand, and I gratefully accept it. "Yeah, pretty much. He just wants some kisses."

With his strong grip, he pulls me to my feet, steadying me as I regain my bearings. "Does he typically stay inside or outside?"

I dust off the butt of my jeans. "He's totally fine being outside during the day. He prefers that, actually. His energy is endless and it's good for him to be able to run around all day so that when I bring him inside in the evening he's less apt to destroy everything you know and love inside your home. At night he sleeps in a crate, so you won't have to worry about him roaming through the house getting into things or anything like that."

"How is he with other animals?"

We naturally gravitate to walking the inside perimeter of the fence. "Indifferent, which is surprising, I know. Your cat is inside, I assume?"

He rubs his hand along the scruff on his face. "Yeah. Milo isn't a fan of dogs, or *anyone*, just so you know. Maybe we should avoid having them run into one another. It shouldn't be an issue, though. He tends to stay hidden in the *cata*combs."

"*Cata*combs?" I eye him.

"Yeah. Lined with human skulls and everything."

I roll my eyes. "You're ridiculous. *Cat*acombs would more likely be lined with the skulls of mice."

"Nope. Milo is savage. Definitely all human. I'll give you a tour sometime."

I stuff my hands into my back pockets. "Pass, but you should probably give me a tour of the rest of the place."

"I can do that."

We slowly make our way back inside, and my anxiety suddenly and unexpectedly wraps me up in a fucking bear hug. *Great.*

It's not because of the situation or anything specific that triggered this feeling, it just comes out of absolute nowhere sometimes. In my mind I can be fine, but my body's reaction to whatever chemicals are fucked up in my brain tells a completely different story.

I focus on taking deep breaths, trying not to make it obvious as he leads me through the halls pointing out each room as we go, and shows me how to arm and disarm the security system. He shares with me all the details of Sienna's day and night routine, his voice filled with love and adoration for her. My heart pinches and I'm so glad this sweet baby found her way to him in such a sad situation. I hope her mom chokes, wherever she is.

"My schedule is pretty flexible because almost all my classes are online. Which I am sure you already know because as *my professor* it's likely you have access to my schedule, no?" I give him a flat look, half teasing him about the fact that he failed to divulge that bit of information. He doesn't even look guilty about it, so I continue. "I go in person once a week, but that class doesn't interfere with the schedule you sent me. I'm fine doing school while I'm here, and I promise it won't hinder my ability to care for Sienna and give her all the attention she needs. I'm a great multi-tasker."

He pulls out a seat from the island now that we're back in the kitchen. "I trust you." There is a stretch of silence. "And it's definitely not because I had a friend run a thorough background check, asked all of your former employers how you were with their kids, and have cameras in every room of the house."

I laugh incredulously. I guess the fact that he's taken these steps also saves us an awkward conversation about the skeletons I haven't exactly chosen to keep in my closet. "I would expect no less." I take a seat, leaving an empty one between us. "You're sure you're fine with me just coming and going even while I'm not working? I don't want Kronk to be a burden to you, but I also don't want to be a bother being here to take care of him day and night."

He pulls a key from his shirt pocket and slides it across the granite countertop. "It's a non-issue."

Something in his tone catches me off guard. I need to get it together, because there's no way he *wants me here,* wants me here. I take the key and close my fingers around it. The jagged edge bites into my palm. "Anything else I should know?"

"I think that covers it," he seems thoughtful like he's searching the files in his mind for anything he may have forgotten to share with me. "I'm sorry about your dad."

The sentiment comes out of nowhere, but I appreciate it

nonetheless. It's not something we can or should continue to tiptoe around. I give him a tight smile. "Thanks."

"You have my number. If anything comes up, I'll do my best to answer right away." I'm glad he doesn't press the subject any further. I don't want to have to pretend to be sad.

I press my lips together and nod my understanding, curious if he only means while I'm with Sienna or if he's insinuating that he's happy to be a shoulder for me to cry on as well. I'm not about to tell him I don't have any tears left to shed, but I am considering what other excuses I could come up with to talk to him outside my allotted time with her.

I'm also curious how much we'd have to talk about. He has to be at least a decade older than I am even though he doesn't look like it. I briefly question if my attraction to him has anything to do with my *daddy issues*. That very well could be the case, but recognizing it doesn't change the fact that he is super fucking attractive.

He stands, exuding a quiet confidence that holds my attention without any effort on his part. And it's not just his looks; it's the way he listens, the way he seems to value our conversations, and how he appears genuinely interested in what I have to say.

He looks at me like he can see what I am thinking. His gaze carries a weight that is slightly unnerving. It makes my heart beat a little faster, which is annoying because I literally *just* breathing-exercised it into submission like five minutes ago.

I wonder if my eyes reflect the same interest I see in his.

8

HIS GIRLS...

QUINN

ADJUSTING to Sienna's daily routine has seriously been such a breeze over the last few weeks. My new little nugget is a tiny ball of sunshine in human form—always giggling and flashing her cute gummy smile. She was already a pro-level easy baby before I came into the picture. It's like she was born to just chill and enjoy life.

Grammy, as Jack affectionately calls his mom, cared for Sienna while he was at work up until I came into the picture. It wasn't meant to be a long-term thing, but Jack says she loved babysitting and claims it keeps her young, despite the fact that as much as she adores Sienna, she has a really hard time keeping up with her endless energy and general baby curiosity.

She can't walk yet, but I wouldn't be surprised if she found a way to dismantle the entire house board by board if given the opportunity to try.

The not walking part probably won't be the case for much longer, because she seems to be the kind of baby who hits all their milestones just a little earlier than others, based on what Jack had told me. She is *so* freaking smart for an eight-month-old, and finding new ways to keep her entertained is such a fun challenge.

She naps like a champ, so splitting my time between her and schoolwork is super simple, which is my current situation.

Dealing with CRIM is becoming increasingly frustrating. I'm constantly tempted to ask Jack for help or study tips or *something*; it's starting to feel like I might not make it through the semester otherwise. I've never struggled in any of my other classes before, and I don't want to come across as boasting, but I know I'm intelligent. This is just a completely new and unexpected thing for me. Still, I don't bring it up to Jack again because our relationship is already complicated enough with him being both my professor and boss. I remind myself it's only two more months. All I have to do is scrape by.

The tension between Jack and me has grown, an unspoken connection lingering in the air every time we're in the same vicinity. I am here a lot during my off hours caring for and playing with Kronk. I often catch Jack watching us with a bemused look on his face. I can't quite figure out if it's because he's entertained by our endless shenanigans or if he's just as confused about his feelings for me as I am about mine for him.

I have to force myself not to melt into the floor under his attention.

It's a constant dance of half-smiles and lingering glances, a magnetic pull that feels both exciting and terrifying.

He wasn't exaggerating about the house being utterly

unsettling. I highly doubt it's haunted as he claimed, but there are definitely some creepy sounds that come from it. Probably because it's old as fuck.

With my laptop open on the coffee table, I glance over at Sienna sleeping peacefully on the couch next to me. Her tiny body is sprawled out, one arm framing her head, and her little chest rises and falls with each breath. I gently stroke her soft hair before resting my hand on her. I know I should have put her in her crib, but I feel so much more at ease keeping her close.

My mind has always been consumed with intrusive thoughts about death, and they have never really bothered me. In a way, death is like the male lead in a really good romance novel—dark, mysterious, and inevitable. It's the only certainty in our chaotic lives.

But taking care of this small, delicate baby amplifies those thoughts tenfold. Every move and decision I make feels like it could have life or death consequences and I vividly picture things like me dropping her while coming down the stairs or her just, yanno, stopping breathing.

Do all parents experience this overwhelming fear and doubt? Not that I am her parent, but I definitely have some parent-like responsibilities.

My mind is elsewhere—teetering somewhere between counting Sienna's respirations, the bloody crime scene being described on the screen of my laptop, and the call I got from the detective in charge of my dad's case this morning.

They arrested someone last night—the second arrest so far—and they are confident that several more will follow soon. Both suspects so far have been students, and the authorities believe that the rest of those involved were as well. They're hoping to get one of them to admit to something or point them in the direction of others who tagged along, but so far they've said approximately nothing.

The investigation has been a slow grind, mostly because the small-town police department just doesn't have the resources. It took them over three weeks to make the first arrest because they're working with a skeleton crew and struggling with budget issues. This means forensic tests and other crucial investigative steps have been delayed.

We still haven't even gotten the final results back from his autopsy, only his cause of death and significant injuries, and that was only because those things had immediate implications for the investigation.

One other major issue was the surveillance footage from the parking garage. It would've been a big help, but the cameras had been disconnected just beforehand and now there's a gap in the evidence there.

Despite this, investigators were able to gather some important details from other sources. Witnesses and security cameras from nearby businesses helped piece together a timeline and identify suspects who were around when the murder happened.

The break in the case came when forensic analysis matched some items found on one of the suspects with evidence from the crime scene. This included distinctive marks on their clothing and personal items that matched descriptions from witnesses. Plus, investigators found damning evidence on the suspects' phones, including incriminating texts and location data.

With these leads, they've made their arrests and are now working on getting more information from the suspects. They're hoping that by pressing them hard and using the evidence they've collected, they'll be able to uncover more about who else was involved.

They seem confident about the leads they're pursuing, but they've kept some details under wraps. Because of the ongoing investigation and my personal connection to the victim, they can't disclose much more. They've stressed the need to keep certain information confidential to avoid compromising the investigation and to ensure that the case is handled with the necessary discretion.

I've been reassured multiple times that they are determined to do everything they can to close this and are working hard to ensure that campus remains a safe place for the rest of us.

It's all very strange to me. When I think of my peers rebelling, I think of things like graffiti or like, smoking weed for the first time. What college kids casually commit a murder for funsies? Maybe they didn't think it would result in his death.

Regardless, I am unconvinced.

As for my own safety, I do have a slight sense of unease that comes and goes. Even though the police think the suspects might just be students, I know that there's more to this, but that's not information I am willing to share with them; that there was a deeper, more calculated motive behind their actions—one that likely involved them being paid a significant amount of money to carry out the hit on my father.

I would be stupid not to be suspicious that they also

aren't in any hurry because they know where this trail they are following will eventually lead, and I have no doubt that some of the police department's pocket's are thoroughly lined with Assembly money.

The idea that these students might have been hired and promised something they'll never actually benefit from adds a whole new layer of anxiety for me, because there's someone else out there—or *a group of someones*—who could still be a threat and probably won't ever even be tied to the case.

Not knowing whether or not this is something they will drag me into is driving me insane.

I don't hear Jack enter the house. He isn't supposed to be home until later, which is why his sudden appearance in the living room scares the shit out of me. I let out a loud screech that wakes Sienna, and I feel so freaking guilty about it.

She, on the other hand, is an absolute angel and just looks confused for a moment before flashing me her two-toothed grin.

She sits up in a sleepy daze and reaches for me. Scooping her into my lap, I wrap her up in a bear hug. "I'm so sorry baby. Daddy scared me to death."

Realizing now that her dad is home, her small body suddenly jolts. I jerk my head back to keep from being butted in the chin as she scrambles off my lap. Her eyes are wide with excitement when she spots him.

He prowls across the room like he's on a secret spy mission. This must be a game they play because she kicks her feet like she knows exactly what's coming.

When he reaches us, he falls to his knees and picks her up with a hand under each of her arms. He raises her above his head and then back down again when he smothers her fat baby cheeks with all the kisses.

She giggles maniacally and I kind of feel like doing the same. "You're home early."

He continues his assault but pauses to respond. "Yeah. Canceled the rest of my classes for the day."

I bite back a comment about how nice that must be. I'm only a little salty about the fact that the rest of us still have to do the work assigned. For someone who is such a beast of a professor, he's awfully casual about just not having class. I give him the benefit of the doubt. "Are you sick?"

"Nah." He sits Sienna on the rug and slides one of her toys to her. "Just missed my girls."

I guess seeing Sienna so giddy to have him home makes it a *little* more acceptable. The fact that he has been caring for her full time alone for so long also explains his curtness with his students. I can imagine that I might type out a super short response to something too if I was in the middle of feeding her or changing her while trying to stay caught up on emails and grading.

But...

"Girls?" I raise an eyebrow and the plural-ness of the word.

"Ah." He hesitates. "Yeah. Sienna and Milo."

"Milo is a girl?" I thought the cat was a boy, but I've only seen the dark grey fur ball in passing. He—*she* is easily spooked. Kind of like Kruz. I suppress a laugh at the thought. Kruz *is* as jumpy as a fucking cat.

"Mmm, yeah." He rubs at the back of his neck and stands. "Anyway. We need to go costume shopping. You're free to go for the day," he hesitates. "Unless you'd like to join us."

My stomach dips and I can't name the exact cause. I wish he'd have just asked me to join them instead of throwing the option out there like that. The rejection sensitive dysphoria is real. "I dunno. Shopping with this girl seems like a blast, but I have this professor who is kind of a hard ass, and the paper he assigned this week is eating me alive."

No point in sugarcoating it. He already knows I think his class sucks, even if I originally divulged that tidbit of information unwittingly.

"What's it on? Maybe I can—" It registers mid-sentence that I'm talking about him and his jaw clenches. "I am *not* a hard ass."

I look at him innocently.

"You seriously think I'm a hard ass?"

"Perhaps this is simply a 'it's not you, it's me' situation again."

He's unconvinced I mean that, and he should be because I don't. It's definitely him.

He's thoughtful for a second. "Take a break, go shopping with us. I could use the help, Sienna is a handful."

I close my laptop and stand, releasing a breath. "Is that an order, boss man?"

"I don't *order* you."

I pick Sienna up from her place on the floor and prop her on my hip. She smacks her toy against my chest as I look him up and down. "Change out of whatever that is and I'll get this one ready to go." I'm just fucking with him—he actually looks a little *too* good. The white button-up he's wearing clings to his frame, accentuating every bulge and curve of his taut muscles. I'm sure his ass also looks amazing in the slacks he has on, but I definitely don't notice that.

The look on his face is priceless.

"Wait, what's wrong with what I'm wearing?" He's genuinely concerned.

I ignore him and continue walking toward the stairs, biting my lip to keep from grinning even though he can't see my face now.

He must realize I'm joking, because he calls after me, "I was going to offer to help you with your paper after, but I guess that was against my better judgment."

I turn back to him. "It's fine. I'll just use my nanny dollars to pay for a tutor or something."

He looks incredulous. "Oh, come on. My class is *not* that hard. You don't need a fucking tutor."

"Fuh fuh fuh fuh fuh," Sienna emphasizes each syllable with a smack of her toy against my chest and I don't even try to hold in the laugh that breaks free this time.

9

UNINVITED

QUINN

WE TAKE Sienna to this super cute shop in town because Jack is insistent that she needs an insanely overpriced Halloween costume.

What he actually said was something along the lines of, "Wally World doesn't have anything we like." As if she's not less than one years old and will be wearing it for more than like forty-five minutes.

The store is on a cozy little side street paved with cobblestones, and it's all decked out for the holiday. There are jack-o-lanterns on either side of the door and fake spiderwebs all over the windows.

Jack has Sienna's carrier strapped around his waist, but when he takes her out of her car seat she immediately reaches for me. "Daddy came home early just to spend time with you, sweet girl. Aren't you tired of me?"

The corners of her eyes glisten as big crocodile tears form, and Jack gives me a pained look. "I've been replaced."

"You have not." I roll my eyes and take her from him

because I care way more about stopping her tears than I do about his hurt feelings.

He unclasps the carrier and readjusts the band, his fingers deftly navigating the straps. I'm closing the car door when he takes me by surprise, coming in behind me to wrap it around my midsection.

His sudden closeness catches me completely off guard, the gesture is both far too intimate and surprisingly comfortable. *Familiar.*

His hand rests on the small of my back for a moment longer than necessary, and when he finally steps back, there's a lingering connection that doesn't require physical touch on either of our parts. His eyes catch on mine, and it feels like a silent understanding between the two of us that the effortlessness of whatever *this* is—it's not something that either of us can easily ignore.

Chill bumps rise on my arms in response to his nearness, and he must notice because he opens the passenger door and pulls out my jacket... which he then proceeds to help me into. Thankfully there is a bite in the air I can blame—though that's not the reason at all for my sudden shiver.

A bell tinkles as we enter the shop and my nose is immediately filled with the cloying smell of pumpkin spice. The shelves are stacked high with jars of pumpkin-scented candles—several burning—competing for attention with displays of fall that have thrown up on every available surface.

I *am* a pumpkin spice girlie. I love fall and all the scents and flavors that come with it, but this is a lot.

But because candles are my favorite thing ever, I can't

resist stopping to smell a few. When I pop the lid off the third one, Sienna grabs for it wanting to join in on the sniff test.

"Like this." I make a show of holding it up to my face and taking a deep breath through my nose, then I hold it a safe distance from hers to see if she'll do the same.

To my surprise and delight, she does. It's both adorable and hilarious, especially when she gives me a look of disgust. "Yeah, I don't like that one either." I giggle.

I notice that Jack is staring at us with what can only be described as affectionate curiosity, but I force myself to not hold his gaze for too long. "I think the burnt sugar and leather scented one is my favorite," I tell Sienna, as if she has any idea what I am saying. Even so, talking to babies is important.

I screw the lid on and place it back on the shelf before moving to follow Jack to the side wall that's lined with tiny Halloween costumes.

Amidst the mass of them, Jack's gaze immediately fixes on a tiny red lobster outfit. He pulls it from the rack and it's complete with oversized googly eyes and two foam claws. "Look no further. This is the one."

I cover Sienna's eyes and he looks at me confusedly. "You're serious?"

"Dead."

Sienna shoves my hand out of the way and giggles. "A lobster?"

"Oh, absolutely. This will be perfect for handing out candy. I can make her walker into a giant stew pot."

"Jack, you cannot be serious. Of all the hundreds of fifteen dollar costumes available anywhere else, you come here to spend seventy-five on *that*?" I point at it like it's offensive because it *is*. "Also, what do you mean 'handing out candy?' You're not taking her trick-or-treating?"

"Quinn, she only has two teeth." He completely ignores my protests about the costume.

"Almost three and that's not the point. She would have so much fun."

He makes a beeline toward the cash register before I can continue to try and talk him out of buying it. "I guess I could walk her around the neighborhood once," he relents, pulling his credit card from the slot in his wallet to pay for this monstrosity. "If you'll come with us."

He doesn't look at me as he says the words, and I am thrown off balance. I open my mouth to respond, but close it again as I try to formulate a response. I am really overthinking this. I am Sienna's nanny. Surely it's not weird for me to be involved in a milestone for her, like her first trick-or-treat?

The broken parts of me often long to be wanted by someone, and it's very frustrating that the most recent someone happens to be Jack, who I should not have these kinds of feelings about for so, *so* many reasons.

I try really hard to hide my distaste with his purchase because the lady behind the counter is not on my side. "Such a cute choice. Your baby is going to be absolutely adorable."

It takes my brain a second to realize that Jack has disappeared to somewhere else and she's talking to me. "Oh I'm not—"

"She *is*, isn't she?" Jack interrupts, popping back up beside me, nearly causing me to jump out of my skin. "We're going as Ariel and King Triton," he announces. The thick glass bottom of a candle clacks against the countertop as he places it there for her to ring up with the costume.

I'm too dumbfounded to form a retort so I force a smile and kiss the top of Sienna's head instead. I would love to take her trick-or-treating, Jack's presence and desire to have me there notwithstanding.

"Why not Prince Eric?" the lady asks as he swipes his card.

He does not hesitate with his response. "Oh, I would *definitely* be her daddy." He winks and takes the bag as she awkwardly slides it across the counter, speechless.

Just like me.

When we're back on the sidewalk I finally find my voice. "I don't remember agreeing to wear a clamshell bra as part of my job duties."

He snorts a laugh. "You're telling me you don't want to see Kronk in a Flounder costume?" That would actually be really cute. "*Or* me without a shirt?" He flexes his pecs.

"Oh my god, you're such a dork." I slap him playfully on the arm and open the car door to put Sienna back in her seat.

She's all tuckered out from the short trip, and once she's all strapped in she's already nodding off. "Baby girl likes her car seat, doesn't she?" I let the *daddy* comment slide because I honestly don't even know what the fuck to say to that.

"She's pretty happy just about anywhere."

I hum thoughtfully. I think the only time I've seen her almost cry was a few minutes ago when she wanted me. I rub the top of her head. "I love her so freakin' much."

I turn to find Jack's eyes transfixed on my back. He snaps

out of whatever reverie he's lost in and gives me a lazy smile. "Me too."

10

ACID REFLUX

QUINN

THE NEXT DAY I arrive at Jack's house to an eerie stillness that isn't typical for a weekday morning. The usual sounds of him up and about preparing to leave for work are absent when I enter through the front door.

I make my way to the laundry room first, plagued by a sense of anxious dread that I can't shake. Part of my routine is to take care of Kronk before I switch over to nanny duties, but the dog crate that we agreed to keep in here is empty.

I open the back door and quickly scan the yard. My perusal pauses when my eyes land on where I left Kronk's food and water bowls a few days ago. The utilitarian setup has been replaced with a white oak dog feeding station shaped like a fucking bone. His silver bowls are nestled in their respective openings and I have to do a double take because, for the love of all things canine, there is a literal battery-operated clip-on fan attached to the edge. Despite how ridiculously heartwarming this would be any other time, the yard is also empty, and a lump forms in my throat.

I suck in a deep breath and try to center myself; I am overreacting, this is just my anxiety. Jack probably took Kronk for a walk, it's fine. Not something he has done before that I know of, but it is the only explanation I can think of that doesn't make me want to cry.

I can't settle until I know for sure, so I race quietly up the stairs and peek into Sienna's room to find her still asleep in her crib. That helps none at all because Jack wouldn't have left her alone to walk Kronk, so there's a solid chance that Kronk somehow figured his way out of the fence. My heart beats wildly at the possibility of that.

It likely goes beyond a comfortable level of propriety, but I close Sienna's door and make my way to the end of the long hallway where I know Jack's bedroom is. I'm in such a panic I forget to knock and realize a second too late that he could be naked or something in here, fresh out of the shower since it *is* time for him to leave for work soon.

That's not what I find.

Jack is sprawled out on top of his big, poofy comforter, Kronk laying on his arm with his head on a freaking pillow. There is a puddle of drool by his snout, and neither of them stirs.

My dog is apparently not a very good guard dog. That coupled with the fact he's never met a stranger he didn't consider his best friend should probably be cause for concern.

I am not sure who I am more jealous of; Jack because he is sleeping with my dog—which is something I have never been able to do—or Kronk because he's pressed against Jack's hard, shirtless body.

My gaze wanders over the shelves of books that line the

walls. Most catch my attention with their bland titles, centered around criminal psychology, serial homicide, and other macabre subject matter. Probably not bland for someone who doesn't study those types of things day in and day out, but very fitting given Jack's profession.

I can't help but wonder if he ever reads for pleasure and if he does, what type of books he's interested in. It's probably not werewolf erotica, but I'm sure we have other things in common. Maybe Poe? I am versatile like that.

The sound of Sienna's morning babbles fills the room through the monitor on his nightstand, and my eyes are drawn to the thing next to it that looks suspiciously like a sex toy. This suspicion is confirmed by the bottle of lube next to *that*, and I did not need to know what type of assistance my professor uses when he strokes his cock.

This is not an image I need in my head, and I am going to replace it with something more savory.

As soon as I think of what that might be that would suffice.

Sienna's cute baby sounds are more than enough to wake him. He is bleary-eyed as he attempts to sit up in bed and realizes Kronk is still passed out on his arm. He spots me witnessing their entanglement and is momentarily surprised.

"I thought you'd be up by now and panicked when I couldn't find Kronk. I'm sorry, I'll just—" I start to step out, but at the sound of his name Kronk pops up and hops off the bed to come to my side.

Jack rubs his eyes, then gives me a sleepy, sheepish look. "I felt so bad for him sleeping in that crate, all uncomfy with no pillow."

Jack loves hard, which is a scary thing because I'm growing attracted to more than just his looks. "He can't have a pillow because he will eat it."

"I know, I know. But he didn't try to eat mine, so that's a plus." He slings his legs over the edge of the bed and stands, his corded hamstrings pulling my eyes directly to them because he's only wearing boxers.

This is not helping me to stop imagining him touching himself.

Kronk tippy taps around my feet, signaling that he's ready to go outside. "I'm going to let him out and I'll grab Sienna."

"Thanks, I've overslept."

I would probably oversleep too snuggled up to this warm fuzzy boy. I scratch the top of Kronk's head and turn to leave, but he has other plans.

He hops back up on the bed and off the other side, snatching the stroker from Jack's nightstand and trotting back over to me with it like he wants to play fetch.

In his defense, it really *does* look like a dog toy. Maybe not one that Kronk has ever owned, since I usually buy him horse toys—those are the only ones he doesn't destroy right away. But still, it definitely resembles a dog toy.

Jack panics, following quickly behind him, and when I instinctively go to snatch it from Kronk's jaws, he grabs my bicep to try and stop me.

A sudden jolt of pain courses through my arm, causing a prickling sensation that lingers. I recoil from him, wondering why it hurts so much. I have a small raised scar near my shoulder from when I had a lipoma removed as a child. I don't remember the surgery because it was very minor and so long ago. It has always been irritating, but never painful.

I try to hide the fact that anything is amiss because I don't want him to feel bad for accidentally hurting me in his panic —it's not like he grabbed me all that hard—but he isn't paying attention anyway because now he's playing tug of war with my dog and his sex toy is the rope.

"Kronk! *Nech to!*" Jack surprises me with the Czech command.

I can't stop myself from smiling, and Kronk releases it immediately, sending Jack stumbling backwards a few steps before he regains his balance and very awkwardly chucks the toy into his bathroom and slams the door shut before my dog can chase after it.

"I'll just—" I am trying *so* hard not to laugh. I jerk my head toward the exit so Kronk will follow me. "Yeah."

I duck out, closing the door behind me, and Kronk barrels down the staircase like a maniac, wearing a path in the hardwood on his way to the back door.

I am thankful to be outside for a minute because inside was... a lot.

I take only a moment to regain my composure because I need to grab Sienna, and I arrive at her bedroom door just in time for Jack to step into the hallway half-dressed, buttoning his pale blue dress shirt. He proceeds to roll up the sleeves at his forearms and I stand frozen because I need him to not do that.

His demeanor has completely shifted from mild embarrassment to complete nonchalance, so I guess we are going to ignore what just happened.

Fine by me.

For now.

I make a mental note to tease him about it later.

"Need something?" He is the picture of innocence but I feel as if there is an evil smirk hidden beneath the layer of ingenuousness etched on his face.

There is no way he doesn't know what he does to me. He probably has this effect on everyone. Is he being extra hot on purpose? Because if so, that's fucking rude.

"Nope." The word comes out more strangled than I would like, and I am thankful for the feral scream that Sienna releases to let me know I'm taking too long.

My mood shifts when her sweet smiley face comes into view, and it's easy for me to push the other thoughts aside. While she is the reason for our forced proximity, she is also a very good buffer.

I change and dress her, and by the time we make it to the kitchen for breakfast, Jack is nursing a steaming cup of coffee. I suppress a groan and I'm not sure if it's because of the smell of coffee or the fact that he hasn't put his jacket on yet and I can see the outline of every muscle in his back when he turns away from me to grab his toast that's just popped out of the toaster.

With Sienna resting on my hip, I turn away from him and head to the other side of the kitchen where her bottles and formula are. I mix one up quickly. As I wait for it to warm up, I sense Jack's gaze on me from across the room, his eyes boring into my back as if reading my inappropriate thoughts.

Sienna twists her fingers in my hair and when I look down at her she's smiling up at me like I'm the only other person who exists in the world. I kiss her forehead and gently pinch her chubby cheek. "I love you, pretty girl."

I take her bottle from the warmer and pop it in her mouth. She accepts it greedily and when I finally turn to face Jack again, there is a softness in his expression that causes a fissure to open somewhere deep in the left side of my chest.

To be adored by a parent is not something I am familiar with, and regardless of my age, the longing has not lessened over the years. My thoughts go to my mother and how visiting her now might mend the broken parts of our relationship, but I remind myself that I was not the one who damaged it to begin with and it is not my responsibility to fix it, especially not simply because she's on her death bed.

I will stick to the daily calls I make to her nurse.

Those are sterile. Manageable.

I need therapy.

I force a smile despite the tightness in my throat, and he clears his.

"Hey, are you feeling okay?" He walks toward me and rests the back of his hand against my forehead. "You're flushed."

Yeah, that happens when I feel like I could vomit. Usually when I think about either of my parents. Particularly lately. "Yeah, I'm fine."

Sienna interprets this as playtime. She coos and smiles around the nipple of her bottle, milk dribbling from the corners of her mouth.

We are crowded against the counter, and I am thankful to have her between us. Jack's presence is suffocating, his large frame filling the space, his nearness sucking out all the air. A familiar warmth crawls up my throat.

"Is it okay if I take Sienna out for lunch today? I thought it might be good for both of us to get out of the house for a bit." I abruptly change the subject to the first thing that pops into my head and focus on feeding her to avoid his gaze.

He steps to the side to retrieve a travel mug from the cabinet next to my head and I hold in the sigh of relief that threatens to spill from my mouth. "Sure. I'll leave my car for you."

My face twists in confusion because he already installed a car seat in my car in case of emergencies. "Why would you do that? How will you get to work?"

"I would feel better if you took my car." He grabs his keys from the island and holds them up, making sure I see where he's leaving them—as if it would be an issue for me to find something sitting right in front of my face. I stifle the urge to roll my eyes. "I'm already late, I'll hitch a ride with Ezra."

I recognize the name because Ezra Birkner is also one of my professors. "That seems like an unnecessary inconvenience for both of you when I have *my* car to take."

"It's no big deal. We carpool often." He's not looking me in the eye now, seemingly preoccupied with filling his mug with coffee while simultaneously typing something on his phone—a text to Professor Birkner, I assume.

Yet, I can't help but feel that he is deliberately trying to avoid looking at me, and then it dawns on me. "You think my car is unsafe."

Come to think of it, Jack has had everything I could possibly need delivered since the day I started. At first I thought it was because he was thoughtful, but now I am wondering if it might be because he doesn't want me to have to drive her anywhere.

He opens the fridge and pulls out a container of creamer, still not making eye contact. "No. I *know* your car is unsafe."

"It is *not*." I am genuinely offended. I worked hard to save up all five thousand dollars I paid for that car. It was my first real grownup purchase. I realize it's not the nicest, but it is reliable and I have it serviced regularly.

Now he looks at me. "Quinn. If someone hits you in that thing, there's a solid chance it'll end up a twisted hunk of metal."

Sienna is finished with her bottle now. I place it on the countertop more roughly than I intend and the sound of it smacking against the granite cuts through the space between us. "It was a Consumer Reports top safety pick, *thank you very much.*"

"Yeah." He puts the creamer back in the fridge, wholly unaffected by my small outburst, and turns to face me. "In 2005."

I release a sound of indignation. Sienna takes it as an opportunity to take my bottom row of teeth into her tiny fist and yank downward. I gently remove her hand and kiss her fingers. "My jaw does not unhinge, cutie girl. Quinny is not a boa constrictor, but thank you for trying."

Jack snorts a laugh as he comes over to kiss her chunky cheek before heading toward the door. "Take my car. I'll see you both around five."

The door closes behind him and I'm left to stew in my own annoyance. I'm charmed that he is so attentive and caring, but that doesn't stop me from wanting to stop somewhere for window chalk so I can draw a giant peen on his back window.

My car is *fine*.

And whatever the slime that's oozing and swirling in my stomach right now, it's not because I'm smitten.

It's hyperacidity.

Or something.

11

CHIVALRY, OR SOMETHING

QUINN

HISTORY OF PSYCHOLOGY is my only in-person class this semester. I've always been incredibly thankful that in my four years at Cypress, most of my classes have been available online. It's what has allowed me time to juggle going from one full-time job to the next.

While I appreciate online learning for the flexibility, it's kind of refreshing to be in a classroom once a week. Actually getting to see faces and have real discussions is a nice break from the virtual grind of monotonous lectures and neverending assignment lists.

I can't say I don't feel sketched out at times when I am in person, because I have no idea which of my peers may or may not have had something to do with my dad's murder.

As a postgraduate next semester, I won't have the option to remain mostly online—which will make holding down a fulltime job on the side fairly impossible—but I will have *Daddy's money* at that point and I'll be able to live quite comfortably through both my master's and PhD.

Sometimes I consider leaving Cypress for the rest of my education. Not because I don't love it here, but because I feel anxious to be as far away from reminders of my father—and those who seem to still worship him—as humanly possible once this school year ends.

But leaving academia is not something I ever intend to do and staying in Hallow is more than ideal when I don't consider all the baggage I have accumulated over the years. It's been my home for my entire life, and if nothing else, I find a small amount of comfort in the familiar.

Thinking of the future gives me a sick feeling that has never been there before, and I am certain that it comes from knowing that once I move on to the next portion of my education, I will also have to move on from Sienna. And as much as I don't want to admit it, Jack.

I know this is ridiculous because I have been with them for such a short time, but when I hear Jack's booming laugh from around the corridor the sick feeling turns to something more heated and *tingly*.

It reminds me that being in his space for only a semester and a half is probably for the best.

I steel myself because I have no choice but to pass by him to get to the exit I'm heading toward. I don't know why I'm so nervous but interacting with him in this setting feels strange. Saying hi and moving on is not an option, mostly because I want to know what he's doing here and who is with Sienna. I assume her Grammy, but I am curious nonetheless.

Our schedules align perfectly which is part of why this particular job was a no-brainer, so I'm not surprised when I turn the corner and find that, per usual, she is strapped to his chest.

If I'd wanted to slip by without them noticing, I wouldn't have had a snowball's chance in hell because Sienna spots me from a mile away and lets out an ear-splitting screech that causes everyone to stop and look in their direction.

Jack has a perplexed look until he sees me walking toward them. He smiles widely when he spots me and I nearly melt into a puddle of goo on the floor.

I have *got* to get it together.

"What are you two doing here?" I take Sienna's hand once I approach them, hoping it will suffice in calming her down, but it's no use and Jack knows this too.

He wordlessly unclips the sides of the carrier, allowing me to slip her out. "I needed to grab some paperwork from my office."

"Ah." Sienna is content with her head on my shoulder, and I sway her from side to side out of habit. "The agreement you signed to wring the absolute most out of each of your students?"

He shakes his head in mock annoyance. "You know, you're the only one who complains."

"Everyone else is probably scared of you because you're so intimidating. I'm the only one brave enough to tell it like it is." I am not intimidated by him at all.

"Is that so?" An unruly strand of hair dances in front of my face. I go to brush it away, but the tips of his fingers beat mine there and he gently tucks it behind my ear.

There is no awkwardness in the gesture, but he shoves his

hands in the front pockets of his pants as if it will keep them from doing anything else without his permission.

Sienna pops her head up, fighting sleep as babies do, and plants a drooly kiss on the edge of my jaw. "It's past your nap time, girlie pop." She gives me the smuggest look within her baby capabilities like she knows she's gotten away with something.

Jack reaches to take her from my arms, but she does not intend on going back to him. She just lays her head on my shoulder again and ignores his existence.

I comb my fingers through her silky brown hair. "Quinny will be with you all day tomorrow." She curls into me harder.

He places a hand on the small of her back. "Does Quinny want to put Sienna in her car seat?"

"Of course I do." I go to adjust the strap on my bag and realize I've left it *and* my laptop in the classroom. "Shit. I need to go back for just a second. I left something. Sienna, go to Daddy so Quinny can be quick."

She's too tired now to protest much further and returns to Jack easily this time. "We'll wait here for you."

Sunlight streams through the glass double doors, and I don't realize how much warmer I'd grown standing in the exit area with Jack and Sienna until I turn the corner to head back to the classroom. I reenter the dimly lit hallway, and the cold, damp air hits me in the face. The contrast is jarring, causing goosebumps to rise on my arms. It's part of the charm of Cypress; how some parts of the school feel like you've stepped back in time.

The chill seeps through my thin sweater. I hug myself and keep my gaze fixed on the stone floor ahead of me, in so much of a hurry that I don't realize I'm about to smack into someone until it's too late.

"Oh my god, I am so sorry." I curl my fingers around his biceps to steady both of us. He is vaguely familiar, and the look on his face tells me he's going to be an asshole about the fact that I should watch where I'm going.

I mean. He's not wrong.

He jerks away from me like my touch might burn a hole through his sleeves. "Too wrapped up in thinking about how you'll spend Daddy's money next?"

I scoff and skirt around him. I've danced this dance too many times to count, and this douchebag is not worth my time or mental energy. I'm not going to try and convince him or anyone else that what they think my life is like couldn't be further from the truth. It doesn't affect them and I don't know why they care so much about it.

I guess they're too bored of their own lives, and the fairytales of this town aren't enough to keep them occupied so they spin their own.

"I guess Daddy isn't enough to keep you at the top of the class now that he's gone, is he? I didn't think you needed any additional advantage but I see you're sucking Hollis's dick to stay ahead now too."

Yes, because god forbid a man ever admits a woman is capable of a level of intelligence beyond his own. His words echo off the walls and I'm thankful the hallway is empty.

Or at least I think it is, but I turn to face him again and see Jack standing just behind him completely *staggered*—and growing more irate by the second—as Sienna snoozes away in his arms.

That doesn't stop me from fully intending to hand this prick his ass but he shoves his foot even further into his own mouth before I have the chance to respond. "Since you're lining up to suck cock, you can get on those pretty knees for me while you're at it. Seems like a good way for you to pay your dues like the rest of us who haven't been given a leg up like you have."

He doesn't realize we aren't alone and I don't give him any indication otherwise. I straighten myself and cross my arms over my chest. "Whip it out then." I make a show of running my gaze over him. "It'll take what? Two seconds at most. And I doubt you have much to choke on so it shouldn't be too difficult, though I'm not sure what you think it is that *I'm* getting out of this."

Jack makes a strangled sound like he's choking on air, and I can't hold back a snort of laughter as the man in front of me suddenly looks like he's seen a ghost.

Or maybe eaten a mouthful of shit, not sure which.

He flushes red, starting at his neck and spreading up to his cheeks.

I tap my foot. "What, you don't like an audience?"

He opens his mouth, but nothing comes out and it pisses me off even more that the simple presence of another man is what puts a damper on his boldness. It's taking everything in me not to knee him in the balls.

Jack must see it written all over my face. "I came to tell you she fell asleep." He's gathered his composure, and ignores that there is anyone else present, but the tone of his voice is not one I've heard from him before this moment. "Adrian, could you please grab Miss Ivor's bag from Professor Scott's classroom." He doesn't take his eyes off me—as if I am the one tethering him on this side of not making any stupid, job-threatening decisions—but it's obvious who he's talking to.

We stand outside the classroom, and Adrian fumbles with the knob before quickly sliding inside. The cinnamon toast cunt reappears a moment later, breathing shakily as he hands me my bag. I can see the tension in his body as he avoids eye contact with either of us and attempts to rush away without a word.

He makes it less than two steps. "Mind if we chat before you go?" Jack asks so casually that his apparent mood shift gives me whiplash.

"I have class—"

Jack cuts him off, completely ignoring him. "Quinn, could you please put the baby in the car while Adrian and I have a word alone?" He hands me his keys before shifting Sienna's sleeping form into my arms.

I open my mouth to retort, to tell him that I don't need him and I can take up for myself *because I can*. But the words don't make it out before he wraps his arm around Adrian's shoulders and turns away from me, steering him into the empty classroom.

The heavy door clicks shut and I realize I'm dismissed from the situation. I am equal parts annoyed with the amount of testosterone I was just forced to bask in, and glad that for once I don't have to deal with such a fucking jerk myself.

It's exhausting.

By the time I have Sienna snug in her seat, Jack is already approaching.

"That was... fast." I gently close the car door and thankfully when it snaps shut, Sienna doesn't rouse. "You know I can—"

"Yes, I know," he cuts me off and holds out his hand. I realize he's asking for his keys a beat later and I drop them into his waiting palm. "But you shouldn't have to. Do you need a ride to your dorm?"

Terseness is not something I am used to from him, and I don't like it very much so I am terse back. "I can walk."

I expect him to push, but he responds with a curt nod and I can't help but feel like he's leaving something unspoken.

There is a bit of tension between us now because of the super uncomfortable situation we were just in, but I know it will dissipate. "Thanks."

I turn away from him and head toward the dorms.

I hope he knows I don't just mean for the offer of a ride.

12

FUCKING SPIDER GUTS

QUINN

IT'S a torrential downpour outside the night before Halloween. A deluge of rain hammers against the window panes of my dorm room, drowning out the muffled sounds from the hallway. I watch the torrents of water slide down the glass, distorting the streetlights into wavy orange blobs before pulling my focus back to the text in front of me.

Sitting cross-legged on my bed, I balance my book on one knee. The faint scent of cedarwood drifts through the room, courtesy of the flickering candle on my nightstand, the flame casting dancing shadows across the pages.

The sporadic sounds of laughter and the occasional shriek pierce through the stone walls, overpowering the steady drumming of rain. Despite the chaos of other students acting like they've never experienced a power outage before, I am determined to maintain my focus on studying for my exam.

As long as I don't set off the fire alarm with my makeshift

study setup, I should be able to avoid the wrath of the douchey dorm room authorities.

The textbook is for Jack's class, so my evening has been filled with eyeballs full of gruesome crime scene photos and detailed reports of serial murder investigations. Not ideal for a night alone in a supposedly haunted dorm, but 'tis life.

My life anyway.

I am tempted to send him a miserable-looking selfie of me studying for his class, but opt not to because I need to reserve my cell phone battery.

Kruz doesn't have the same concerns because she left to stay with her parents the first time the lights flickered.

Kruz: You know you can still come stay with us.

It feels so weird to me to stay with anyone else's family. Probably just another of the many effects of my childhood trauma, but she still offers despite the number of times I've refused for various reasons.

Quinn: I am fine here. It's quiet and I'm using the time to study.

Someone squeals outside my door and the sound of footsteps pounding down the hallway as they run away makes me a bit of a liar.

Kruz: How are you not scared?

Quinn: Of the dark?

Kruz: Of the possibilities of what could happen in the dark.

I really don't know how she gets through the day most of the time. I laugh and roll my eyes.

Quinn: You are seriously so dramatic.

Somewhere in the middle of reading about the social

characteristics of a particularly disgusting serial killer who enjoyed peeling off his victims' skin and frying it up like bacon, my eyelids grow heavy and my head droops.

I jolt awake to complete darkness, the candle having burned out leaving me disoriented in the disconcerting silence. I don't know if minutes or several hours have passed, but it seems to be the latter.

I fumble in the dark to re-light the candle, and a sudden coldness settles in the air, making the hairs on my arms stand on end.

I swat at something crawling on my hand and lift it in front of my face, inspecting it in the dim light.

Fucking spider guts.

"*Gross.*" I wipe the offending hand on my comforter.

From the edge of my bed, a strong grip clamps down on my wrist and jerks me off it, nearly dislocating my shoulder. If I thought Jack grabbing my arm the other day hurt, that I was nothing compared to this. My body slams against the hard floor with a thud and I release a loud scream, instinctively flailing and fighting against whoever the fuck has balls enough to do something like this in the dead of an overly silent night where anyone and everyone will hear.

"Shut the fuck up," the voice unmistakably belongs to Adrian, and for the first time in a really long time, I am actually scared.

Before I can react, he kicks me hard in the ribs, knocking the air out of me and silencing my screams.

I try to fight back but his weight is on top of me now, straddling my hips and covering my mouth with his hand to muffle any other sounds I might make to draw attention.

He's bigger than I am, but not so much bigger that I am unable to give him a fight. I buck my hips as hard as I can, catching him off guard and gaining enough space to flip onto my stomach and shove myself to my knees. I try to scramble away but before I can fully escape, he grabs a fistful of my hair and yanks my head back, pressing something cold and metal against my bared throat.

I must be fucking stupid, because I hadn't even considered he might have a weapon until this moment.

"What the fuck do you want?" I grit out, my heart threatening to claw its way out of my ribcage.

"Oh, I think you know." He slams my face into the corner of my nightstand and the last thing I'm cognizant of before everything goes black is my candle smacking against the floor and rolling toward the open door.

WHEN I FINALLY REGAIN CONSCIOUSNESS, I gasp for air, jolting upright. My eyes adjust to the dim light, and flick nervously to the candle still burning on my nightstand.

Jesus Christ.

Relief washes over me as I suck in deep breaths, trying to calm my racing heart. *What the fuck kind of nightmare was that?*

I fumble around the bed, trying to find my phone in the tangle of sheets so I can see what time it is. My fingers finally close around it, but when I tap the screen, nothing happens. It's dead and won't be able to charge it anytime soon because the power is still out.

I groan and blow the candle out because it's been burning for long enough that it's a fire hazard at this point, then wrap my blankets tighter around myself. Typically I would be able to drift back to sleep quickly to the sound of the rain outside, regardless of whatever mental gymnastics I just did in sleep, but something scrapes at the edges of my mind.

My thoughts involuntarily wander to my parents and the lack of their presence in my life up until these last few years, particularly these last few months. My dad's voice still echoes constantly in my head even though I haven't heard it since our meeting at the beginning of the term.

I can't say I miss it.

The fact that his case is still open is something I desperately want to put behind me. It fuels this relentless anxiety that has consumed me lately, apparently even in my sleep now.

Every second I spend in the quiet of my head sends me spiraling, and I'm thankful for the busyness of the majority of my days outside the walls of this haunted dorm room.

Thankful for the busyness of Sienna.

For the distraction of Jack.

And in this panicked state I'm struggling to come down from, I find that right now, all I want is him.

Most of the time the only ghosts are the ones in your mind, but that doesn't make them any less terrifying.

13

MY RESTRAINT IS CLOSE TO SNAPPING

JACK

SIENNA IS SO VERY ATTACHED to Quinn.

Understandably, because so am I.

She's flush against Quinn's chest, snuggled close in her wrap. Her little arms flail excitedly as Quinn gently sways back and forth in an attempt to settle her a little before we make our way down the first street.

A look of pure love and tenderness is written across her soft features as she coos something about all the candy Sienna will get tonight and how she wishes she would have thought about getting a pumpkin for her to paint.

It slaps me in the face daily that Quinn treats Sienna like she is her flesh and blood, and this is one of those moments. She has natural maternal instincts that cannot be forced, and I want to tell her how much it means to me that my daughter has her in her life, but that feels like too much too soon.

Everything about her feels like too much too soon, particularly the *certainty* I felt the moment she fell into my lap.

The certainty that roared through the rush of blood in my ears: *mine.*

I've never been one to ease into things, and my restraint is close to snapping.

The street is buzzing with kids running around, laughing and yelling like little psychopaths, their costumes flitting behind them in the fading light. Some hold their parents' hands while others tail their older siblings, all eager to skip to the inevitable upset stomachs they'll have in a few hours.

My chest feels tight when I consider how it was once a possibility that Sienna may have never had the opportunity to experience this. How it would have been so easy for her to have missed out on what it's like to just be a kid. Anna's decision to allow me the privilege of being her father was the best choice she could have made for her while struggling with active addiction.

It hits me often how different Anna is now. We were so close as kids—inseparable, really. I don't know when or why things changed, but somewhere along the way, she veered down a path I couldn't understand. The little girl I used to love, who had such an innocent spark, living this broken, miserable life. It tears me apart—it's like watching a part of yourself fracture, and you're powerless to stop it.

Sienna lets out a yelp and it slices through my despondent thoughts. I look up to see her grinning at me, her tiny legs wiggling manically, drool spilling from the corner of her mouth. If she could say many words, I'd have been certain that was just a, "Hey!" Her little lobster Halloween costume looks just as ridiculous and adorable as I knew it would.

My gaze flits to Quinn using the end of her sleeve to clean Sienna's face. I couldn't convince her to go for the full mermaid getup, which is a damn shame, but our matching Little Mermaid shirts are just as photo-worthy. Even if things don't end up going the way I hope they do between us, I'm glad for the little family photo shoot we had before coming out. I've already made a picture of the three of us my phone background so I can see her as often as I want, even when she's not around.

Not that I don't spy on the real thing on my security cameras while I'm at work.

Unfortunately she's not always at my place.

I briefly muse about how I could possibly sneak a camera into her dorm. The fact that I am even considering that should sound several alarm bells, but the sad truth is... I am not sure I'd even hesitate if given the opportunity. Nor would I feel bad about it afterward.

She feels me looking and her green eyes meet mine. I don't think I've ever noticed a single other person's eye color, but they're the most stunning shade of olive and I can't help but stare. She smiles and it makes me want to kiss her stupid.

Holding back the words I want to say is impossible.

"You're such a natural with her. The little mama we've been missing." I place my hand at the base of her back as I lean across them to grab Sienna's treat bucket from the car's front seat and close the door. "What will we do without our little mermaid when you've moved on to bigger and better things?"

I don't want to think about that and I don't know why it's

the first thing that came to mind. *Maybe because you just threw yourself off the deep end with that mama comment, you fucking moron.*

It's not the save I hoped it would be.

Her mouth gapes, like I've rendered her speechless which I am pretty sure is a hard thing to do. She's such a puzzle to me, a seemingly open book but somehow I feel like there's something about her that I'm missing.

I want to know everything there is to know about her.

"There's nothing bigger or better than this one." She brushes Sienna's sparse hair back. "And I don't want to think about that right now."

That makes two of us. Perhaps I'll just keep my stupid fucking mouth shut now.

We walk in silence toward the first house, but as the elderly woman who lives there fills Sienna's pumpkin bucket with an excessive amount of candy, Quinn leans in close to me and finally speaks again.

She's standing on a step above me, putting her more on my level than she normally is. Her breath still smells like the cinnamon latte she had on the way here, and her mouth's proximity to my face nearly undoes me. "I hope you know you're enough for her."

I'm unprepared to hear those words, but I know she must be saying this because I used the M-word. I press my lips together in a fine line and nod once.

I think most days I do know, but there will always be a part of me that is sad for what Sienna has missed out on that I can't replace.

"I didn't have either of my parents growing up," she

admits after we've said our thanks and begun to walk away. "But my aunt was enough."

I have always suspected what kind of man her father was. I think most people in Hallow do to some extent, but I never imagined that she wasn't even raised by her parents. Something in my gut tells me their abandonment of her isn't something she shares with many people.

Most everyone assumes their relationship was something more than what it apparently was. Hallow is a small town. People talk—more than they should and most of the time they don't have a fucking clue about what they're saying.

"Do you see her much now?" I touch the tip of Sienna's nose and for the first time since Quinn has been in the picture, she reaches for me to take her instead.

Quinn doesn't hesitate. She folds down the wrap and slides her out, and Sienna all but leaps into my arms as she releases a string of *da da da das* that make my heart feel like it might explode. "I did until recently. She's older and hasn't been well for a few years now. We still speak on the phone often, but her son thought it would be best for her to be closer to him. I can't say I disagree, but it sucks not having her nearby. He's several years older than I am and not as wrapped up with school or work. His job is fully remote, so he can be there for her in ways that I'm not able to be. I hope to visit over Christmas break."

The thought of her spending Christmas or any holiday anywhere that isn't with us doesn't sit well with me, which is a ridiculous notion because she has her own life. I have to remind myself that this is just her job.

But that's the thing, isn't it? The way she is with Sienna. It's *not* just a job for her.

"Anyway. I do kind of hold a grudge against my parents that I'm sure I'll heal from someday, but I grew up loved and cared for even if my home situation was unconventional. I'm thankful that my aunt wanted me when no one else did. If I could go back and choose, I would have still chosen her."

The words hang heavy in the air, and as Sienna rests her head at the base of my throat I find myself hoping like hell that someday she'll be able to say the same for me.

The rest of the evening blurs by, and before I know it, Sienna's bucket is filled to the brim.

On the ride home, my chest still feels tense with lingering emotions from the unexpectedly deep conversation between Quinn and me. I grip the steering wheel a little tighter in an attempt to ground myself.

We're barely a mile from home, but Sienna is asleep before we even pull up the drive. Thankfully, her costume is too thick to be worn safely in her car seat, so she's already in a fresh diaper and onesie when Quinn carefully transitions her from the car to her crib.

I'm anxious for her to come back down. I want a few moments alone with her before Ezra and Stu interrupt us, which is a funny thought because we've had this annual Halloween thing for years and really she should be considered the party crasher except she is not that at all. I want her wherever I am at all times. I haven't mentioned to her that I am having guests over, *or* that I want her to stay.

With every fiber of my being I want to do something that crosses that line of professionalism, just to test the waters and see how she reacts. I just can't figure out how to bring it up without making things weird.

But I'll beg if I have to.

Unfortunately, I don't get the opportunity. The incessant ringing of my doorbell tells me Stu has arrived first.

14

FUCKING COZY

QUINN

SIENNA'S EYES popped open for a split second when the doorbell started ringing, but she quickly drifted back off when it stopped.

I assumed it was a late trick-or-treater, continuously pressing the doorbell in hopes of snagging some last minute candy or pranking the spooky house on the corner. But when I head downstairs a few minutes later, I hear Jack's stern daddy voice, scolding his friend for being so loud when he knew the baby was already asleep.

I wish he'd use that voice on me. *The things he could get me to do with it...*

I wasn't aware he was expecting company and I am slightly disappointed. There is an insistent part of me that always wants a few extra minutes with Jack, even after my job responsibilities have ended for the day.

Sienna too, honestly.

Leaving either of them is hard.

Their hushed voices echo throughout the space and I am

slightly nervous at the prospect of meeting his friends, even though it was bound to happen sometime or another with how often I am here. I don't know why I feel anxious about it, it's not like I am his girlfriend... just the nanny.

The living room is filled with laughter and the scent of a candle burning on the mantle. When I look closer, I realize it's the same candle I was looking at while we were Halloween shopping, and it makes my stomach flip. Even though the little pumpkin has gone to bed, it's clear that Halloween is still alive and well in the Hollis house.

Jack and his two friends are lounging on the couch with drinks already in hand. He notices me and motions for me to join them, patting the spot next to him.

"I should get back to my dorm," I say, all while walking toward him regardless. My mind says *leave*, but my body has a mind of her own. "Yanno. Avoid my car getting egged."

He takes my hand and pulls me down next to him, far too close and too comfortable for a *nanny* to be sitting next to her *boss*, or a *student* to her *professor*.

We have been a bit too comfortable with one another from the beginning, I think. But, he's never been so forward like this. Especially not with other people around.

My eyes dart to his friends, anxious if they're judging, simultaneously wondering what the fuck has gotten into him between five minutes ago and now.

Not that I mind.

I recognize Professor Birkner—Ezra—from campus; his long limbs stretch out in front of him, his inked forearms peeking out from under the sleeves of his hoodie. He's got this casual, scruffy charm, like he doesn't care much about appearances. Everyone swoons over him to a ridiculous extent. I can see why people would be drawn to him—he's got that artsy, too-cool-to-care aura—but he's not my type. Maybe if I were more into guys who give off a fuck boy vibe—or guys at all—I'd give him a second glance, because he is definitely attractive.

More Kruz's type, to be honest, but I don't think she'd ever fraternize with a professor.

I never imagined *any* of my professors would be my type, *or* that I would want to *fraternize* with them, but here we are.

Ezra gives me a bland smile that I return.

Next to him, grinning from ear to ear, is someone I don't recognize. He's equally as tall, though a little more lanky, with a mess of blond hair. He seems to vibrate, his sharp jawline and bright blue eyes holding my attention for a beat too long. The corner of his mouth twitches.

He scoots over to me with exaggerated enthusiasm, nearly spilling his drink in the process. "Fucking cozy. I like it."

I snort, dodging the sloshing liquid, but still find myself shoved even closer to Jack than I was before.

Jack pushes at his shoulder, forcing him away from me. "Fuck off, Stu."

"Party pooper," he whines, scooting back to his original spot.

"I'm not a party pooper, you're just fucking annoying," Jack replies, adjusting himself to give me a little more space.

I get the impression now that maybe he immediately pulled me down next to him as a form of protection from his friend's lack of respect for other people's personal space.

"I feel like I'm intruding," I admit, moving to stand again. "I'm gonna bring Kronk in and say goodnight."

"I forgot about the dog," Stu is ecstatic. He stands and heads for the back door without waiting for a response, "I'll get him," he yells over his shoulder.

Jack tugs at my hand. I don't know what's gotten into him, but I really like it. "You're not intruding. I love having you here."

I feel a blush creeping across my face at his compliment, coupled with his possessive tone that is more endearing than overbearing, and I realize two things at once.

One, Jack is staking a claim on me in front of his friends. He is making it abundantly clear to them that I am something more than just his nanny.

Am I?

Maybe he just wants his friends to lay off his nanny? I dunno.

But I do think that's something we've both known from the start, though what even that *something* is doesn't quite have a definition yet. At least not one we've spoken out loud or given a name to.

Two, I don't think I mind.

I'm going to let him.

I kind of like it.

Okay, that was more than two things, but you get the picture.

But wouldn't he have already told them if he has a thing for me? Do dude bros talk about this kind of stuff? *Does* he have a thing for me? Am I reading too much into this?

Wishful thinking?

With a loud thud, Kronk bursts into the room and rushes towards me. His paws hit my chest as he jumps, knocking me off balance and causing me to tumble awkwardly onto Jack's lap. I struggle to catch my breath as Kronk bounds onto the couch and smothers me with slobbery kisses all over my face.

I expect Jack to scold Kronk for jumping on me, or at least for jumping on the couch; that would be the normal thing to do. But instead, he throws his head back and laughs, twisting my body toward his and pulling me closer to his chest to shield me from Kronk's playful assault.

I love that he doesn't mind how doofy my dog can be. Kronk and I have always wrestled around with each other like this, and I love playing with him, so it means a lot that Jack enjoys his crazy energy too.

After a few minutes of wrestling with my dog, who refuses to give up the game, Jack finally convinces him to hop down. "That's twice now," he says with a grin, scratching Kronk's neck with one hand while the other stays wrapped around my waist. He's referring to the two times Kronk has knocked me into his lap. "Good boy."

I twist my head to get a better look at his face and the room seems to shrink to just the two of us.

Ezra stands from his place on the couch and pads off to the kitchen. The movement grabs my attention and I come to my senses. Thank god, because I really wanted to kiss him just now. How fucking awkward would that have been?

When I finally peel myself away from Jack, I find Stu leaned against the doorframe holding a freshly poured drink, watching us with curious eyes.

The tinge of embarrassment I should feel for being

caught in such an intimate moment with my professor doesn't come.

I plop down on the floor next to Jack's feet and wrap my arms around Kronk's furry body, giving him a squeeze. He's less excitable now that he's gotten past the initial sight of me, and he lays down next to me, resting his head on my thigh.

Jack squeezes the back of my neck. "You'll stay, then?" he asks.

"For a bit," I reply.

"Good." He brushes my hair from my face and stands. "I'll grab you a drink."

Stu pushes off the wall and follows him into the kitchen, and I am left alone for a few minutes.

It's nice being here with Kronk, hanging out inside like a normal girl who has a normal living situation with her dog. I wish it could be like this every day.

To prevent myself from thinking too hard about any of this, I pull my phone out and look over an assignment while waiting for them to return.

I've checked out when they finally come back into the living room, and I am absentmindedly scratching the top of Kronk's head while reading over some mock case notes when Jack takes his seat on the couch behind me. He reaches around me to hand me a drink. When I snap back to reality, I find that his thighs are on either side of my shoulders.

Great. How am I supposed to not drool now? Maybe I could blame the drool spot on Kronk.

"Are you seriously doing homework?" He twists a strand of my hair between his fingers and I have to physically restrain myself from leaning into his touch.

"These blood spatter patterns are fascinating." I hold my phone up to show him, as if he isn't the one who gave me the assignment to begin with.

"Okay, Dexter. Calm the fuck down," Stu interrupts, visibly cringing.

Ezra just snorts.

"Stu can't handle blood," Jack tells me. "Him's just a widdle baby. It makes him all queasy," he says teasingly.

Stu glares at him as I close out the screen on my phone and stick it back in my pocket.

"You can have your blood and guts, I'll stick to malware and firewalls."

Ezra ruffles his hair. "Your work is just as important for crime prevention, buddy."

He beams, flashing us the caricature of a proud face, then says, "Too true. Also, I would like to thank Quinn for being the only person in your academic circle I've met that hasn't attempted to make me pass out with whatever gross shit she was just looking at on her phone."

"I would never," I laugh.

"And you are alone in that," Ezra says proudly.

"So mean," I lean into the couch cushion—into Jack—as I down the rest of my drink.

"So many unwanted images seared into my brain." Stu shakes his head as if he's trying to rattle them free.

"You should see the real thing sometime," Jack teases. "An entirely different experience."

"Yeah, hard pass," he replies. "I'll stick to clickity clacking on my little keyboard, thanks."

"I guess that means you won't be joining us on our trip to

the body farm next month." Ezra claps him on the back. "You'll have to miss out on all the fun things we have planned."

I suspect he's just teasing him further, because the body farm isn't open to visitors, even from other universities. I know because I've looked into it.

"Fun for *you*. I'd be the guy puking, crying, and dying in the corner."

"Lame." Ezra slouches further into the couch. "I can't wait to get up close and personal with those ripe, decomposing bodies—maybe even take a deep breath and savor the blessed scent of science in action."

Stu dry heaves and Jack and Ezra both laugh loudly, confirming my suspicions.

"We'll be sure to bring smelling salts if you change your mind," Jack offers.

Stu just flips him off.

I am *mildly* buzzed from drinking whatever Jack just handed me so fast, and while I have been trying really hard not to laugh at his discomfort throughout this conversation, I find myself wanting to play along now too.

"I can't believe you guys didn't invite me," I say with a frown. "I don't wanna miss out on watching those cute lil' maggots wriggle through half decayed flesh. I don't think I'd ever feel as at home as I would while up to my elbows in rotting cadavers."

Jack squeezes my shoulder, giggling as Stu gags again, takes a deep breath to steady himself, and downs his drink. "Fuck all of you. I thought we were going to be friends," he says to me.

"I mean, you're *their* friends." I gesture between Jack and Ezra.

"Yeah but they're assholes and they team up on me. Where is *my* teammate?"

"Look elsewhere," Jack says, banding a possessive arm around my chest and resting his cheek on the top of my head.

I decide I want to tease *him* too.

"I'm sorry, Stu," I say. "Bad first impression. What can I do to make it up to you?"

It's like he reads my mind, because the look on his face is pure mischief when he responds. "I *do* need a date for my sister's wedding next month." He raises an eyebrow.

Jack goes completely still, and his body's reactions tell me everything I need to know.

I understand now why his attitude toward me has been so different with them here—why he felt the need to stake his claim.

Stu seems like he might just be a big ol' flirt.

And while I initially did want to tease Jack a little and I *do* think Stu is harmless, I can't bring myself to respond to him in any kind of way that might make Jack feel like I am interested in anyone but him.

Because I am most assuredly not.

"In your dreams." I give a breathy laugh, and the words aren't even fully out of my mouth before I feel Jack relax again.

It makes me want to giggle and kick my feet and scream into my pillow.

Stu must have zero sense of self preservation, because his

response causes me to chuckle and Jack to heave a throw pillow at his head. "Every night, pretty girl."

The rest of the evening passes with me trying to leave several times and Jack insisting that I stay for multiple card games, which I assume is what old dudes do for fun these days because I've never played a game of rummy before in my life until tonight.

Ezra's reserved and moody demeanor is day and night from Stu's unpredictable and freaking *hyper* personality. Jack, on the other hand, seems to fall somewhere in between the two and they both seem endlessly entertained by him, as if he's a playful puppy they adopted somewhere along the way, but I suppose that is how a lot of friend groups fall into place.

It's close to midnight when they finally say their good-byes. I wave them off and head to the upstairs bathroom. There are multiple on the main floor, but I can never resist checking in on Sienna one last time. I need to take the longest breath I can before heading home myself. I have not peopled this much for a really long time, and I am peopled *out*.

I lean against the cold wall next to baby girl's bedroom door, regather myself, then head back downstairs.

15

A TORTURE I'M WILLING TO ENDURE

JACK

I WONDER if she'll try and bolt once the guys leave, but I could use one last drink and I'm guessing she could too. She seems to be just as drained from social gatherings as I tend to be.

I quickly put Kronk in his crate for the night. He gives me a sad puppy look that tells me he expects the bed treatment indefinitely and I feel a pang of guilt. Tomorrow I'll hook him up with a fillable chew toy stuffed with dog-safe peanut butter as penance. "Not tonight, buddy."

When I'm back in the kitchen, I hear her footsteps descending the creaky stairs, and I call out her name to let her know where to find me. When she enters the room, I already have two glasses of wine poured and sitting next to Sienna's treat bucket on the island. Our relationship may push the boundaries of propriety, but all I care about right now is keeping her here with me.

She eyes me curiously, her gaze flitting between me and the glasses of ruby liquid on the counter space between us.

"Someone has to eat the candy." I shrug and slide the bucket toward her. "Kronk is all settled."

She releases a small breath of laughter before uncrossing her arms and walking over to take it. "Okay, but all the candy corns are mine."

My face pulls into a grimace as I follow behind her, carrying our drinks into the living area. "Fine by me."

"Don't tell me you're a candy corn hater." She plops down on the couch and unceremoniously dumps the candy out on the cushion next to her.

"It's literally corn syrup-flavored wax." I take the seat on the other side of the pile of treats, simultaneously hating and thankful for the space between us.

I've already been more up close and personal with her than usual, but I couldn't help myself. I knew exactly how Stu would treat her if I didn't mark my territory.

Fuck.

Mark her.

Blood rushes to my ears at the thought.

And to other places.

I shift uncomfortably, readjusting myself as I recite the pledge of allegiance in my mind.

When I look at her again, I remind myself of the boundaries that must remain between us—I'm her boss and her professor, and that's all I can be for now. I can't cross that line, no matter how tempting it is. But if she were to make the first move? That would be a different story. Tonight, I pushed the boundaries a little more than I planned, getting more comfortable with her than I intended, partly because I felt a surge of possessiveness while my friends were around.

Despite my intentionally respectful thoughts, I can't control the spark of electricity that jolts up my arm when she takes the glass of wine from my hand and our fingers brush.

The way she smiles, the way her hair falls across her face.

It's a torture I'm willing to endure.

I'm not even going to try and rationalize any of this.

She's still here. That's all that matters.

She takes a long drink before setting her glass on the sofa table and ripping open a small bag of candy corn. "More for me, you big weirdo." She dumps the contents in her mouth and I force myself to pull my eyes away.

I grab the remote and flick the TV on, scrolling until I find some random horror movie I know nothing about because I don't watch them, but it seems fitting since it's Halloween. I turn the volume down low, only meaning for it to be background noise to our conversation.

Her nose scrunches adorably but she doesn't say anything.

"Not a fan?" I hand her the remote.

"Meh." She tosses it to the side instead of switching to something else, then turns her body to face me more directly, pointedly ignoring the screen.

I make a mental note for future reference and shift the topic of conversation. "Finished your paper?"

She snorts. "Yeah, I submitted it last night."

I don't tell her that I know she did, or that I've already read it in its entirety. "Is it really that bad?"

"Can't say I've had worse." She tears open a mini Snickers and pops it in her mouth before reaching for her glass again.

I genuinely don't understand why she feels so negatively about my class, especially not after reading her work. She's brilliant. "The offer still stands if you need to talk anything out."

"Offering your nanny preferential treatment?"

I give her an uneven smile. "I would offer help to any of my students who expressed the need." I probably wouldn't.

She downs the rest of her wine. "And how many of them express the need?"

I don't answer right away, allowing the silence to stretch between us while I finish my own drink and dig through the pile of candy for some Twizzlers.

"Really?" She raises her eyebrows. "And candy corn is bad?"

I bite down and rip off a small piece from the end using my front teeth, then offer the rest to her. She surprises me by biting a piece off too, and I feel like an adolescent because all I can think of is the fact that our mouths just touched the same place.

"You didn't answer my question," Quinn says. I was hoping she'd forget.

"Sometimes," I admit, though that might be stretching the truth and the thought crosses my mind that maybe what she said before is true; that my students don't approach me simply because they think I'm an ass.

I know that I am brusk with them, but it's not because I am the jerk they think I am or because I mean to be dismissive. I just have my hands full with Sienna outside of office hours, but physically cannot leave an email unanswered or an assignment ungraded. Life work balance is definitely something I need to work on. It's a problem for me.

She picks at the end of her hair, avoiding eye contact. "So what you're saying is it's just me."

"That is not what I said." I huff a laugh. "But I have found that most of the time the issues students have with my class typically come from outside stressors." I give her an opening to talk to me if she needs to. I know she has her own friends and family she could open up to, but I desperately want to be that person for her. *Any* person she needs me to be. She seems fine for the most part, but with all she's dealt with this semester alone...

"I'm not stressed," she says, standing to pad back to the kitchen.

She returns with the rest of the bottle of wine and fills both our glasses again. If this is what she needs to relax for a few hours, that's more than fine with me. I can't drive her home if I drink the rest of the bottle with her... but I'm going to drink it regardless, so I guess she'll just have to spend the night.

Something tells me she wouldn't expect me to wake Sienna for the drive anyway.

A glass and a half of wine later, I discover that Quinn is more of a lightweight than I expected. Her cheeks are flushed and she's staring at the TV, but I can tell she isn't registering what's happening on the screen. Her mind is somewhere else.

We've eaten a good portion of the candy; enough that I am reminded why Halloween happens only once a year. When her eyes fall shut, I sweep my arm across the couch, nudging both the leftover candy and empty wrappers back into the treat bucket.

"I wasn't finished with that." She releases a sleepy giggle, her eyes still closed.

I place the bucket on the floor and stand, staring down at her and debating what our sleeping arrangement should be for the night.

I grab a blanket and Sienna's baby monitor from my room, stopping to peek in on her one last time for the night before bed. When I return Quinn is curled up in the fetal position sleeping more soundly than a person should be, being that she was just awake less than one minute prior.

The couch has a chaise lounge on either end, and I decide the most appropriate thing to do is place her on one and me on the other. I could just leave her here and sleep in my bed. That would likely be the normal thing to do, but the way I feel about her is not *normal* and I don't want to be that far from her while she's sleeping under my roof for the first time. If I can't have her in my bed, this will have to do.

I toss the blanket aside and scoop her up, shifting her to the spot I've assigned her in my mind.

What I don't expect to happen is for her to latch onto my arm and pull me down next to her. "Snuggle," she murmurs.

I am a lost cause, and I can't even blame the alcohol.

I am keenly aware that if she were not a little drunk, she would most definitely not be asking me to snuggle up with her to sleep.

Regardless of how much I would love to do just that, it's wrong for a multitude of reasons.

The number one reason being that I am not sure I can

handle so much skin to skin contact without losing my fucking mind. The desire to mark her as mine is almost unbearable even when we aren't touching. I don't even want to think about how she might react to the thoughts I have about her. *Yeah, I want you; and oh hey, by the way can I just like... stab you a little bit? With maybe a small knife? Nothing serious.*

The desire I have to break skin is not something I share with many people, and for the most part I am able to keep it at bay. But every inch of her unmarked body screams at me incessantly and *oh my god I have got to stop thinking about this right now or I'm going to do something I really fucking regret.*

I uncurl her hand from my bicep. "I'll be right here." I pat the section of the couch adjacent to where she is lying and cover her with the blanket.

She murmurs something incoherently and twists her body away from me, burrowing deeper into the cushions. I can't resist brushing her hair from her face, but that has to be the most intimate contact I allow myself with her tonight.

I settle in and stare at the ceiling for longer than I care to admit. I am thoroughly distracted by every breath she takes mere feet away from me, and when I finally doze off I expect to be awoken by any number of things except for what it is that wakes me.

16

THAT'S RIGHT, GIVE IN TO THIS

JACK

I USUALLY SLEEP SOUNDLY, thanks to Sienna's ability to sleep through the night herself. However, tonight I am jolted awake by a noise sometime after two in the morning.

It sounds like whimpering.

My first instinct is to check the baby monitor, but it isn't coming from there. It's coming from the other side of the couch.

Slowly, I fight to shake off the drowsiness and sit upright. My eyes gradually adjust in the darkness. And that's when I see Quinn, her small frame trembling.

She tosses and turns and a knot forms in my stomach. Her breath is ragged and so unlike her usual calm and measured demeanor. I know it's just a nightmare, but seeing her like this still is unsettling and the need I have to fix it is strong.

I stand from the couch and approach her sleeping form, trying my best not to scare her. But as soon as I place a hand on her shoulder, she startles awake with a violent lurch.

"Hey, it's just me." My voice is still hoarse with sleep, and I say the words barely above a whisper as I brush her hair back from her damp forehead.

All the tension drains out of her body, and I can't stop myself from sitting down next to her and wrapping an arm around her.

She stills for a fraction of a second, then completely melts into me. *That's right, give in to this.*

"Good girl. You're okay." I readjust my body to settle us both more comfortably. "That must have been a hell of a nightmare. You scared me to death."

She rests her head on my shoulder innocently and sighs. "Scared you? I'm never going back to sleep now. I don't even remember falling asleep to begin with."

"You asked me to snuggle."

She jerks away from me and looks up at me with her mouth half open, and it's fucking adorable. "I did not."

"You definitely did."

"Please kill me."

"No." I tug her body back into mine and she seems too exhausted to resist. "Look at us, we're snuggling now. You got what you wanted after all."

She glares at me.

I boop her on the nose and it softens the grumpy look on her face. "Do you have nightmares often?"

She doesn't answer right away, but then she says, "Lately, yeah. Usually I'm unphased, but they're just so incessant. And they feel so *real*."

I nod thoughtfully in the dark. "Stress?"

"I'm not stressed." She's still adamant about this, but we both know she's lying. It's even more obvious now.

"Anxiety, then?"

She's reluctant, but she finally admits, "Maybe a little."

"Well. I can offer you two things: a movie marathon for the rest of the night that we'll both regret in the morning or something to help you sleep."

She doesn't hesitate to accept the offer of the latter and it makes me wonder exactly *how much* her anxiety is affecting her lately. From the outside looking in, she seems so calm and collected. If I wasn't aware of the things she's dealing with mentally right now, I probably wouldn't have considered that her nightmare was anything but just that—a nightmare.

We'd all probably feel much better if all the arrests were made and her dad's case closed, putting the lingering fear that's plagued our town firmly in the past.

Lucky for her, I'm hyper focused on everything about her at this point, and am ready and willing to force her to let me help in any way I can.

I reluctantly pull away from her and she flops back onto the couch, staring blankly into space as I head for the stairs to grab my emergency anxiety meds from the medicine cabinet in the bathroom attached to my bedroom. I peek in at Sienna on my way back down, and when I reach the bottom step I question whether or not it's the best idea to so casually give someone else my prescription medication.

I immediately push the thought aside when Quinn comes back into view because there are not many other things in the world I want more right now than to erase that troubled look from her face.

I walk past her and into the kitchen to grab water for her to take the medicine with. I fill a glass from the dispenser in the fridge and make my way back to her. She gives me a weak but grateful smile as she takes the pill from my outstretched hand, not even bothering to ask what it is before swallowing it down with a gulp.

The trust she's placed in me does things to my insides. It's overwhelming in the best way.

I won't take it for granted.

"I was thinking I should fix the guest room up for you." I take the seat next to her again.

She doesn't say anything, just lets her head fall back and releases a small hum of what I assume is agreement.

I explain anyway. "I can't imagine this will be the only time you need to sleep over and the couch is not ideal."

The thought flits into my mind that the room that shares a wall with mine is also not ideal because she belongs with me.

In my bed.

"You could sleep in there now, but no one has been in there in ages." *Or we could skip these bullshit formalities and go straight to the part where you're in my bed.*

What the hell am I thinking? I need to get a grip. It's not fair to her, and this line of thought just makes everything more complicated than it needs to be.

"I'm fine here."

I nod and heave myself off the couch again, taking my place on the other side away from the dizzying feel of her body heat so close to me.

We both lie back down, and I'm more tense now than before. The room is filled with an uneven silence, broken by the sound of her irregular breathing. I wonder if she's still awake staring at the ceiling like I am, or if she's fallen back asleep.

"You're a good friend, Jack." She yawns and squirms around, trying to get comfortable.

Her words hang in the air. We are more than just boss and employee or even student and professor. We are friends. Our connection went beyond mere passing interactions after our second time sharing the same space. Seeing her with Sienna has already planted the seed that there is something more to her—more to *us*. And with her giving a name to it, it solidifies and takes root in my mind, becoming a tangible and undeniable classification.

I was certainly a good friend to her when I helped Adrian fall face first into the corner of a melamine desk a few days ago.

Though, some may have considered me doing such a thing might have been for purely selfish reasons; the skin under his right eye split *beautifully,* and the look on his face when I told him what I'd do if he so much as breathed in Quinn's direction again? *Priceless.*

Naming our relationship somehow relieves the pressure I've felt building; gives me room to breathe again because now I don't have to rationalize the very strong need I feel to care for her in every way.

We *are* friends.

That's what friends do.

Do friends share a bed, Jack?

I mentally berate myself but come to the conclusion that yes, sometimes they do.

And I'm about to become the best friend Quinn Ivor has ever had.

17

A TOOTHBRUSH WOULD BE HELPFUL

QUINN

SITTING UP, I scrub at my eyes and try to shake off the drowsiness. The taut fabric of Jack's couch beneath me reminds me that I'm not in my bed. Stretching my arms above my head, I run my fingers through my messy hair and glance around me. Without Jack's and Sienna's voices echoing through it, the room feels unnaturally large and silent.

The clock on my phone tells me I've slept well past noon, which is so out of character for me. I can't remember the last time I slept so soundly for so long. Whatever medicine Jack gave me last night knocked me right the fuck out.

Probably because pairing sleeping meds with wine is not the best idea, but I don't regret the decision. I've needed to turn my brain off like that for a while now.

The front door opens and I hear Sienna's chatter before she and Jack come into view. He has brown paper grocery bags in each hand, and he doesn't seem to notice that I am awake, because he heads straight for the kitchen.

My eyes are heavy and my steps are unsteady as I

stumble through the entryway and over to the coffee maker. "Please tell me there's coffee," I grumble, taking Jack by surprise.

"Good morning, sleeping beauty."

Sienna kicks her legs excitedly when she sees me, but I pause the half a step I've taken toward her when Jack's cat takes me by surprise, weaving a figure eight around my ankles. She rivals Sienna's demand for my attention in the form of insistent purring.

"Milo, what the fu—frick?"

I stifle my laughter at Jack's censoring of himself and bend down to scratch the top of her head. She leans into my touch and he just stares, obviously dumbfounded.

When I'm upright again, Milo darts out of the room. "What?"

"I'm lucky if he lets me pet him once a month, and even then it's because I've taken too long to feed him and he's trying to bribe me."

I zero in on the fact that he says *he*—as if Milo is a boy when not long ago he told me the cat was a girl.

I am nowhere near awake enough to unravel whatever that ball of yarn is, but I can't stop the feelings that arise at the thought of Jack referring to me as his girl.

Because that's *definitely* what happened, and he *very* poorly tried to cover it up.

I decide to change the subject. "Grocery day?"

I take Sienna from him, and I hope she doesn't somehow sense that it's because I'm using her as a form of armor. I feel less awkward—less anxious—when I'm holding her.

I shift her onto my hip and reach for the coffee pot with

my free hand. The smell hits me in the face as I measure out scoops into the filter.

"I had big plans to make breakfast before you woke up, but we slept half the day too and breakfast turned into lunch," he shrugs, tossing a loaf of ciabatta onto the island.

I nuzzle my forehead against Sienna's causing her to coo. "This pretty girl must have been all worn out from trick-or-treating to have slept for so long."

"Well, we didn't sleep quite as long as you did." *Obviously.* The half grin, half smirk on his face nearly takes my breath away.

Sienna's tiny mouth stretches wide with a yawn, her arms moving to wrap around my neck as she squirms against me. The coffee pot gurgles to life. As much as I want to wait for it to finish and have the time to savor a hot cup, she demands immediate attention. Rubbing her eyes and releasing a whiny grunt, she lets me know she's been awake exactly long enough and is ready for her nap.

"Ready to go night night, pretty girl?" I readjust her on my hip and snuggle her closer. She lays her head on my shoulder in response.

As we start to walk away, Jack's hands freeze midair, holding a carton of eggs. "You're not working today. I'll put her down for her nap."

I wave him off and continue toward the stairs. "As if I need to be on the clock to want to spend time with this sweet baby."

SIENNA'S EYELIDS droop quickly and she's out like a light within a few minutes of being rocked. After gently placing her in her crib, I quietly close the door and return to the kitchen.

Jack is slicing through the ciabatta with a serrated bread knife and the familiarity of our time together last night and this morning almost bowls me over.

Aside from Kruz, I haven't been close to many people. The thought of forming relationships has always filled me with dread, likely because my psyche is convinced no one could ever truly want me.

Thanks, parental figures.

And thanks, in-depth study of psychology, for my astounding self awareness.

The ease with which our connection formed is both surprising and overwhelming.

"That was fast."

Sure fucking was.

But I know he's not referring to what's on my mind. "Baby girl crashed hard." I take my place next to him and turn the stove on, cracking eggs in the pan he's already put oil in.

"How did you sleep last night?" He pulls a toaster from one of the bottom cabinets and places it on the counter, plugging it in before dropping a slice of bread in each slot.

"Much better than I have been lately once you helped get me there." My face burns hot as the words pass my lips, but if he notices the way it sounded to me he doesn't say anything. Maybe his mind isn't as far in the gutter as mine is. "Thank you," I add.

"Happy to help." I don't miss the way the corner of his mouth twitches.

We fall into a rhythm with one another making brunch as the afternoon sun filters through the kitchen window.

This seemingly mundane task of cooking together is more than just making food—there is *something* in the way we are dancing around one another, both physically and in every other way.

I can't help but wonder if there's anything I do that causes him to feel the same desire as I feel when I see his muscles flexing under his fitted button-up shirt. I'm curious if he notices all the different ways I look at him with longing; whether it's when he's with Sienna, snuggling my dog, or just doing things around the house.

I want him in so many different *fucking overwhelming* ways.

He is so hard to read at times, and part of me feels like a silly schoolgirl with a crush on her teacher.

Is that all this is?

Before last night, I couldn't imagine the way I feel ever being anything other than unrequited.

I'm reaching for plates on a shelf inside the cabinet that's just out of my reach when I feel him step in behind me. His hand goes to my hip as he reaches over my head to grab them for me.

The act seems to flip a switch for him just as much as it does for me because once he places the plates on the counter in front of me we just stand there.

Frozen.

His hand still on my body.

I place mine over it and pat just once, a friendly gesture to let him know it's fine.

So fine.

He smells like bergamot, and lavender, and something I can't quite put my finger on but I want to drown in it.

But when I spin out of his grip, instead of moving away he cages me in against the counter.

There is a pained look on his face like it's taking all of his willpower to hold back from doing what it is that he really wants to do.

This should all feel awkward.

Inappropriate.

But it doesn't.

He does something to me that I can't explain. Maybe it's my *daddy issues*, the fact that he's so much older than I am and so caring.

Regardless of the reason, I don't want him to pull away so I return the favor by placing a hand on either of his hips—a silent acceptance of whatever this is between us.

And then I come to my senses, realizing that if this man tries to kiss me right now, I haven't even brushed my teeth today.

Great.

Fuck.

I give him a quick squeeze and dip under his arm.

There is a strong possibility that I have ruined the prospect of there ever being an *us,* but I'm not about to put my lips on his—or anywhere near him—while my mouth tastes and feels a lot like I've chewed on an absolutely rank wool sweater.

"Coffee?" I ask awkwardly, shuffling to pull two mugs out and place them on the countertop.

He clears his throat uncomfortably and gives me a weak, tilted smile that causes my chest to ache painfully. "Yeah, sure."

18

MY BEST FRIEND

JACK

QUINN BLENDS so seamlessly and fits so comfortably into our lives and home regardless of the scenario and it's fucking with my resolve *so* much more quickly than I anticipated. She's wearing me down, completely unaware, and I just pushed a boundary with her I shouldn't have pushed.

I need to fix this.

I promised myself I would let her make the first move then barrelled headfirst into the opposite direction of that promise.

I stand across from her while she pours us each a cup of coffee. I am a respectful distance away when I lean against the kitchen island and face her back.

She turns to hand me my drink and plasters a forced, awkward smile on her face.

I can't say I like that at all.

"I'm sorry," I say—no use beating around the bush or trying to downplay the tension between us. We need to talk about this now before things get even more out of hand.

Her face twists like she doesn't understand. "Sorry?"

"I shouldn't have been so physically forward with you. I made you uncomfortable. It won't happen again." I hope she is not so uncomfortable she's unwilling to stick around. I would kick my own ass if I lost one of the best things to ever happen to Sienna just because I'm a douche and can't keep my hands to myself.

She takes a sip of her coffee and sits it on the counter next to her, then closes her eyes like all of this is just too much to form words about. Maybe she's more upset than I thought.

"Quinn, I promise—"

I'm willing to get on my knees and beg her forgiveness, but she doesn't let me finish. "You have nothing to be sorry for. It's fine. *I* promise." She's refusing to look at me and while I know first hand she doesn't allow anyone to disrespect her, she needs this job and there is a good possibility she'd overlook my shortcomings in order to keep it.

My mug clinks against the stone countertop and I take a step toward her without thinking, then realize I'm doing it again. Boxing her in. She's like a fucking magnet and I need to get a grip.

Why does it feel so right to be drawn to her?

I force myself to take a step back. "I don't want you to be uncomfortable because of me."

She takes in a long breath like she's steeling her nerves, then eats up the space between us as if she needs to do so in order to make her point. "Jack," she says my name like it's her favorite word. "I am *not* uncomfortable. I just don't have a toothbrush here."

The look I give her is one of confusion, because what does that have to do with—oh.

Oh.

I think hard about what my next words should be, and decide that her confession is close enough to her making the first move to me. Or the second. Or whichever fucking one this would be now.

I reach for her hand and she places it in mine, probably not expecting me to pull her into me, but that's what I do.

I reverse our positions until her back is against the counter. She looks up at me, chest heaving. I like that I have this effect on her.

I don't hesitate before I lift her and sit her on the countertop, and she doesn't hesitate to separate her thighs to make space for me between them.

Her neck is level with my face now, just like I hoped it would be.

"That's okay," I finally say, allowing my lips to skim along her skin from her collarbone and up the side of her neck, stopping at the shell of her ear. "I want your mouth, but I don't need it." I place a kiss there to solidify my confession. "I'm happy to kiss you *anywhere.*"

She sucks in a shaky breath, but when I run my hand up the length of her back and thread my fingers through her hair, she relaxes in my arms.

I take my time, kissing along the exposed part of her shoulder and back up her neck again.

What am I doing?

I've completely lost my mind.

But I don't fucking care.

Who needs a mind?

Not me, that's for sure.

There are about a million ways this could go wrong, but I can't seem to think of even one of them with her body pressed against mine and the feel of her skin against my mouth.

"The things I want to do to you." I gently bite down on her earlobe, dragging my teeth over it as I pull away and whisper in her ear. "*Unspeakable* things."

"So do them." Her words come out breathy.

If she only fucking knew. "You don't know what you're asking for."

She's felt so unreachable, so far away for so long—but somehow still a part of me, flowing through my fucking veins.

It is unreal that I have my hands on her now.

Even with the distance I've kept between us, nothing has ever felt more intense or more real than what I feel for her.

I'd let her tear me apart if it meant understanding the grip she has on me—like there's something feral whispering deep inside my bones that only she can bring to the surface.

She reclines on her palms, her head tilted back. I reach out and place my hand between her shoulder blades, pushing gently until her weight shifts forward and she's flush with my chest, then take both her wrists in one of my hands and grip them tightly.

She scoots herself closer to the edge of the counter, wrapping her legs around mine and pulling our centers flush as she grinds her core against my persistent erection.

"You like that?" I ask, thanking every god I can think of that she seems to lean into my dominant nature instead of shying away from it, just like I hoped she would.

She nods.

Grinds harder.

Then realizes what she's doing and I absolutely *do not mind*, but she stills her movements.

"What are we doing, Jack?" she finally asks, a little breathless and a lot needy.

I pepper kisses along her jawline. "I'm kissing you." I don't stop. "Last night, you said we were friends. I'm being friendly."

"Oh." She seems a little disappointed in my answer. "Do you kiss all your friends?"

I smile against the base of her throat before placing a wet, open-mouthed kiss there and squeezing her wrists just a little tighter to get my point across. "No. Just my best friend."

"Oh," she says again.

I'm coming on too strong. I need to calm the fuck down. I pull back from her, unthread my fingers from her hair, and move my hand to cup her jaw. "I'm sorry. I didn't mean to overwhelm you again. I just—"

She brings a hand up to cover her mouth and leans back from me. It's almost comical. "I'm not overwhelmed. I was just hoping that when—if—this happened, I would be an active participant and not just sitting here like a knot on a log."

I smile because she's adorable and most definitely was not just sitting there, but I also understand what she's saying, so I put a few more inches in between us and help her hop down to her feet again.

I turn away from her and readjust myself in my pants. I'm sure she knows what I'm doing, but she doesn't necessarily need or want an up-close view of Jack's erection adjustment just because she was fine with me kissing her.

I turn to face her again and clear my throat. "We can reconvene at a later date. Let me feed you."

Or, I could run out to the store again real quick. Grab a toothbrush. Lube. Several Condoms. Come back and fuck you on every surface of my home. Do that thing I've been wanting to do with my knife.

I plate our food that's now closer to cold than it is warm, so I heat each plate for a few seconds in the microwave before jerking my head in the direction of the breakfast nook next to the bay window.

I'm not certain I can shift back to normal after that, but I'm willing to try and it ends up being easier than I anticipated.

We fall into a conversation about a History of Psychology assignment she's working on this week. Thankfully nothing about our meal together feels strained or tinged with the fact that she just basically dry-humped me while I restrained her and made out with her neck in the middle of the kitchen.

That's okay.

I'll remind her soon enough.

An hour passes and our plates sit empty in front of us, the only thing pulling us from the bubble we've created around ourselves is Sienna's high-pitched shriek reverberating down the stairs.

"I'll grab her." I stand at the same time my phone buzzes from across the kitchen.

I snatch it from the island as I make my way to the stairs,

but stand frozen at the bottom with my hand on the rail when I see the text that's just come through.

The police have made another arrest.

While I should feel relieved by this small piece of news, it's the name attached to the article that triggers a downward spiral of worry.

Adrian.

I can't help but think about the danger Quinn may have been in just a few days ago before I showed up, and the danger she could still be facing now from other students who were potentially involved.

There's not a chance in fucking hell I'll let her out of my sight now. Not until I know for certain she's safe from the same people who killed her dad.

My phone vibrates again, and the text that's come through from an unknown number is the juiciest cherry on top of this shit sundae.

It's a screen grab from the camera system inside my house a little over an hour ago; a still of Quinn's body wrapped around mine, me sucking at her pulse point.

19

I WILL FORFEIT ALL MY MORTAL POSSESSIONS

JACK

IF I THOUGHT I had a thing for her before, knowing there's a tangible threat to her safety now has literally sent me off the fucking deep end. We'd all have been stupid not to speculate that there might be, but according to the information the police have released to the public, all signs point to her father's death being a random act of violence.

The run-in she had with Adrian a few days ago would have been plenty enough reason for me to freak out about her potentially being in danger, regardless of the fact that he is behind bars now. If he was in on this and bold enough to approach her in public in the way he did, who's to say someone else involved wouldn't do the same or worse?

But someone hacking my home security system?

What the fuck?

I fully realize this could just be someone threatening my job and not Quinn.

Fucking around with students is not exactly abiding by Cypress's ethics code, and I am sure there are any number of people in Hallow who would love to see me lose my job—if only for the drama of it.

But, I can't exactly think of anyone who would be lying in wait just hoping I trip up and be willing to go to these kinds of lengths... I am most definitely leaning toward this all having something to do with Quinn.

I'm not saying I want her to move in with me.

Okay. That's exactly what I'm saying.

But how do I word, *I will forfeit all my mortal possessions if you promise to never leave my sight again*, without scaring her off?

I mean. That can't be much scarier than sending her out into the world with a fucking stalker.

One that's not me, that is.

She lingers in the doorway of my study looking like her stomach is in knots. Mine is too, but I refuse to let it show for her sake. I need her to feel reassured that I will take care of this—take care of *her*.

I told her about the text immediately then reached out to Stu. There's no one I trust more to debug my security system regardless of how much of an idiot he is otherwise, not even the security company. Work kept him busy until late this evening, but he and Ezra finally arrived about an hour ago; attached at the hip per usual.

Her gaze flicks to mine, and her eyes are filled with lingering worry mixed with something seemingly trusting. *Loving.*

My stomach dips and blood shoots to my cock because that excites me a little *too* much.

Stu's voice cuts through the waiting tension as he looks

up from the laptop screen he's been poring over for the last hour. "Your security system is pretty basic, but I think it's fine all things considered."

He is the techy one of the three of us, working in cyber security. Though, I've never been a hundred percent sure of what it is he actually does for a living. I feel like that's common for people who work in tech. The rest of us just don't fully understand.

He's good at it, though.

I run a hand through my already-ruffled hair. "Thanks, bud." I look at Quinn again. "You okay, baby?"

The term of endearment falls so easily from my lips, like everything between us has shifted now and I have no desire to backtrack even though this could potentially be a bad idea on both our parts for a variety of reasons.

She smiles and nods. "I'm fine."

"*Daaawwwwww*. You guys are so *cute*." Stu ruffles my hair even more so as he stands from the chair to stretch out his long limbs and I slap at his hand, jerking my head away.

Quinn laughs a little and I'm thankful for his easy way of always lightening the mood.

"Anyways, I think you're all good now but I'm going to set up a connection to my laptop after I rest my eyeballs for a minute so I can be notified if anyone tries to breach it again. Tracking it back to whoever did it the first time was a dead end, but at least now I'll have an eye on it." He heads toward the door, but pauses to say to Quinn, "You should consider staying until we figure this out." He lightly claps her on the shoulder. "The cops aren't going to do shit compared to the protective detail Jacky boy can provide."

His words are laced with innuendo and waggles his eyebrows.

I could kiss him on the mouth for bringing it up first, and I could fall to my knees in gratitude when she nods just once, agreeing that she will consider it.

QUINN

I SNEAK into Sienna's room and sit in the rocking chair in the corner while Jack heads downstairs with his friends to take a break from the monotony of the evening. I'm thankful she's oblivious to all of this and can sleep so soundly, my unbothered baby girl.

I'm staring into the distance when the door creaks open, startling me out of my fucking skin. I have to force myself not to scream.

"Oh my god, I am so sorry," Stu says in a loud whisper. "I didn't know you were in here."

"It's fine," I say, willing my racing heart to calm the fuck down. I feel like Kruz with how jumpy I am right now.

He pads over to Sienna's crib and runs his fingers gently along the top of her head. "Just had the urge to check in on this one."

I kind of want to smack him, because if he wakes her up I am going to have to actually strangle him, but I just smile because I know the urge well.

He shoves his hands in his pockets and steps away from her, then leans against the wall facing me.

"You okay?"

"Yeah," I breathe. "No," I find myself admitting immediately after. "Both, I guess?"

"I get it. I didn't have the best relationship with my dad either."

That wasn't the direction I saw this conversation taking. "How do you—?"

I'm asking him how he knows what my relationship with my dad was like, but he just gives me a cynical snort and closes his eyes, his head falling back against the wall quietly. "I know what it's like for everyone to expect you to be torn up about a family member's death and you're just... *not*, you know?"

"Yeah." *Do I ever.* I'm still put off that he is even bringing this up.

I'm not exactly irritated that Jack has likely talked to him about me—about *this*—but I also kind of am. I haven't even really talked to *Jack* about it much, but I suppose it's no secret and this is not the first time someone has pointed out my apathy in regard to the situation.

Still, it makes me a little sick to my stomach that I shared something so deeply personal about what my relationship with my parents was like and he apparently felt like it was fine to talk to his friend about it. And for either of them to speculate what my feelings in regard to his death have been like? What a person shows on the outside is not always how they're dealing with things on the inside.

Stu is not too far off the mark, but it's still bold of him to assume like this.

Upon further consideration, I probably would have

spilled to Kruz too if the shoe was on the other foot, so I guess I'm a bit of a hypocrite.

"I don't fully know what your relationship with the old man was like, and I know this all sucks and is scary, but you should feel pretty confident that Jack will take care of you until it's a thing of the past."

I just nod. I know he will... and it feels nice to finally have someone in my corner. Jack gave me a job as his nanny during a tough time in my life, and his support has been a lifeline. He's been there for me when I needed it the most; he's become one of the best friends I've ever had.

Maybe more?

It's been more than just a job; it's been a chance to find some stability again during a chaotic time in my life. His support makes me feel lighter.

Being around him and Sienna makes me feel lighter.

"Me and Ez too." He steps back over to Sienna's crib, looking down at her loving as he brushes her hair to the side one last time. "His family is our family."

He exits the room and leaves me in the silence, and I immediately feel guilty for being annoyed with him for saying any of the things he just said.

He's just trying to show he understands and cares—that he plans to be here for me in the ways he can.

I could use more of that in my life right about now.

———

SEVERAL MINUTES after Jack and Ezra have made their way back upstairs, I finally force myself to leave Sienna's room and head down the hall again, thoughts of everything Stu said—everything he's *noticed*—still lingering in my mind.

Back in the study, Jack is ending a call, apparently clarifying something with someone at the security company. His eyes meet mine as I re-enter the room, and that thing happens again; everything else seems to fade into the background and it's just us.

We've barely given in to the spark between us and already I feel utterly obsessed with him.

Stu is back behind Jack's desk at his computer, doing techy things I have no concept of. He asks Jack a question, and I don't hear the words but his voice snaps me back to reality.

Jack rattles off the information, his focus shifting back to the task at hand. I stand by, feeling somewhat useless but knowing that my presence matters. And if not, well, at least I feel safe here with him. I don't think I'll fare well in my dorm tonight, and I'm not sure when I will feel safe being there alone again—or if I will again at all.

I'm definitely not any more useless than Ezra, who is stretched out on the divan playing Candy Crush on his phone.

A silence settles over the room again, broken only by the occasional tap of keys and Ezra's huff when he loses a round. Time seems to stretch, each minute a small eternity as we wait for him to finish up.

I text Kruz, filling her in on the latest episode of the shitshow that is my life. I downplay the severity of it all in hopes that she doesn't freak the actual fuck out.

She does anyway.

Finally, Stu releases a breath and stands again, smacking his laptop closed. "Try and breach *that*, fuckers."

Jack nods and the look on his face is one of gratitude, but at the same time he says, "Cut the camera access, please."

"Not into exhibitionism, then," Ezra jokes, but I don't think he's too far off the mark.

Molten lava settles somewhere around the top of my pelvic bone when I think about what happened between us in the kitchen.

Jack just scoffs. "That's exactly what I meant." He is unashamed. "I know Stu, and him having direct access to my cameras is not my idea of a good fucking time."

Stu just waves him off, "I don't have your cameras on here, dude. I don't wanna see whatever shit you two do when we're not around." He shudders like he's disgusted.

A yawn creeps out of my mouth as he ends the sentence, and I realize exactly how late it's gotten. The entire day and night have gone by in such a blur.

Once they're out the door and it's locked behind them, Jack pulls me against him for a long, much-needed hug. I feel the tension in my body dissipate and I'm suddenly overwhelmed with exhaustion, both mentally and physically.

I guess I'm for sure spending the night again.

Maybe the next few nights.

Or longer.

20

SO MANY UNANSWERED QUESTIONS

QUINN

THE ADRENALINE RUSH of the security threat left me feeling more shaken than I expected it would. But in the quiet hours of the morning, as I lay in bed with Kronk's big head pressing down on my chest like a weighted blanket and Sienna snoring softly from her extra crib next to Jack's bed, I can't help but feel like this is exactly where I'm meant to be, regardless of what brought me here.

After the chaos settled and the guys left, Jack moved Sienna to his room and insisted on bringing Kronk upstairs. It was a simple suggestion on his part, but really poked at the tender parts of my heart. Kronk means the world to me, and it means everything that Jack not only sees how important he is to me but maybe even feels a bit of that connection to him too.

I've shifted in and out of sleep since lying down, never dozing off for more than thirty minutes or so it feels.

Running my hand along Kronk's fuzzy back, I feel so safe

despite everything. My big, doofy emotional support flea brain.

I watch Jack on the recliner in the corner of his room where he insisted on sleeping. His eyes hadn't fully closed until just a few minutes ago. I wouldn't have minded sharing a bed with him, but there is something achingly vulnerable about him like this—his protective nature and the respect he has for the newness of our relationship.

Is it a relationship?

I suppose time will tell, but I wouldn't mind experiencing a little *disrespect* at the hands of Jack, though we both know that wouldn't have been a possibility last night with all the shit happening and his room full of dog and baby.

Still, he stuck to the recliner.

I would have loved to at least tempted him to let go of some of the restraint I hope he's barely hanging onto at this point if he's feeling anything like I am feeling.

My mind replays the events of the night, and I can't shake the feeling that this closeness between us is more than just circumstance.

Sienna stirs in her crib, her tiny hands reaching out for the mobile suspended above her. She'd probably play quietly for a while being the angel baby she is, but I get out of bed anyway, careful not to disturb Jack as I lift her into my arms, cradling her close to my chest. Her nearness is just as much a balm to my frayed nerves as having Kronk nearby is.

Morning light is just beginning to filter through the split in the closed curtains, casting a broken glow across the room. Jack stirs from his makeshift bed despite my best efforts to keep quiet. His eyes meet mine, something unnamed and affectionate passing between us as he rises to his feet. There is a tenderness in his gaze that breaks down every possibility of me keeping anything from him. I don't think I would have regardless.

I will tell him everything about my family over breakfast. I feel like at this point he needs to know the very real possibilities of the type of danger I might be in. Who knows what he might be speculating?

Before I can dwell on the unspoken words hanging in the air, my phone vibrates on the nightstand. I glance down to see a message from an unknown number glaring back at me, the words sending a chill down my spine. If there was any doubt before that Jack's security system being hacked had anything at all to do with me, this completely obliterates it.

He curses under his breath as he comes in behind me, reading over my shoulder.

Unknown: Your dorm room was empty last night. A shame... I just love our visits.

JACK SETS THE TABLE, arranging plates and cutlery in front of our respective seats while I entertain Sienna. She's comfy in her highchair, babbling happily and waving her spoon like a scepter—fitting since she's the queen of this castle.

It's weird having to go on about our day as normal with all the shit that's happened over the last several hours, but I suppose when there's a baby in the picture, they always take precedence regardless of the scenario.

Someone should have told my parents that.

He walks across the kitchen and comes back with a cup of coffee in each hand, sitting mine on the rustic wooden table next to my plate before going back to grab the plate of pancakes he just made for us. Typically, I would have insisted on making them myself, but it was honestly nice to just sit back and watch him work.

"Everything alright?" he asks, taking the seat across from me. He partially peels a banana and breaks it in half, handing the broken-off piece to Sienna. I grin at the way she attacks it and pet the top of her head knowing her hair will be crusted with the fruit long before we finish this meal.

"Yeah, just... processing." My fingers idly trace the rim of my mug. "You're really good at keeping it together, you know."

He makes a sound that is half snort, half chuckle. "I thrive under pressure."

Sienna gurgles in agreement, slapping her chubby hands on the tray of her highchair.

"You put that on your resume?"

He shoves his fork through two pancakes and moves them to my plate. "Yeah. Right beside 'team player and skillful in a variety of positions.'"

The words are laced with a playfulness that is so at odds with the conversation we need to have, but I can't help myself so I match the innuendo. "Easily motivated and eager to learn?"

He's briefly thoughtful before he responds. "*Very* easily motivated with the right employer." The look he gives me is loaded. "Eager to learn, and excellent at giving direction."

I cut off a piece of my pancake, dip it in syrup, and take a bite, chewing and swallowing before I say anything back. I point my fork at him. "You're hired."

He laughs. "This was an interview?"

"You interviewed me without telling me first," I say with a shrug, taking another bite. "Just returning the favor."

He leans across the table and hooks a finger under my chin, pulling my face toward his before placing a soft, sweet kiss on my lips. "Can't wait to get to work."

We are both so freaking smitten with one another that it's hard to keep from falling into banter, but we both realize the gravity of the situation we are in. He sobers before I do. "You've been through a lot," he says gently, and I know he doesn't just mean last night and this morning. "If there's anything you need to put out there..." He trails off.

I sigh, taking a sip of my coffee. The warmth spreads through me, giving me the courage to say what I need to say. My guy has no idea what he just asked for, or what I'm about to tell him.

"I think I know who killed my dad. And it wasn't a random group of students or for no reason." If he's shocked by my admission, I can't tell. "He's been deep into dangerous shit with dangerous people for my entire life. I wasn't exactly surprised that this happened."

Jack's brow furrows. "Care to elaborate?" There is no judgment in the question and he doesn't ask whether or not I have divulged this information to the police like I expected he might.

I haven't and I'm not going to. I don't want anyone else to know, and I don't know if I can even trust them. The last thing I need is to be on someone else's shit list. If they're in The Assembly's back pocket and I go to them with this, I might as well just grab a shovel and start digging a plot up next to Ophelia.

"Yeah," my voice is weaker now. "You've heard people talk about The Assembly, right?" It's a dumb question. Of course, he has. That doesn't mean he takes it very seriously. I feel like most people don't. I probably wouldn't if I didn't know for certain.

He reaches across the table and intertwines our fingers. I don't know if it's a signal that he's listening and willing to hear me out or if he's certain I'm nuts. "I've heard things here and there."

"Well. They're not exactly *all* rumors," I admit. "My dad had been heavily involved with them for as long as I could remember. I've always let on that I was just as oblivious as anyone else..." I trail off. "But even with the limited contact I've had with him since I was younger, it's pretty undeniable. I saw too much and heard too much before my parents ever realized I was old enough for it to register, and even after I moved out, there were so many things that pointed to all that he was involved in. Drugs, cybercrime, bribery. *Illegal surveillance.*" I emphasize that last one because someone having hacked into Jack's security system is five million percent something someone in The Assembly would do.

I just don't know *why* they would do it. What would they even want from me now that my dad is gone?

Jack squeezes my hand, his thumb brushing against my knuckles. "This is all pretty bizarre to hear out loud, I'm not going to lie. But I suspected this or *something* given your history." Finally, his roundabout admission that his digging around had told him more about my family situation than he'd let on, though probably not as much as what I've just shared with him.

It means more to me than I can voice that he's making a solid effort to believe me. "I don't know," I say, doubting everything. "I really don't. But I just have this feeling that he wanted out." And *out* is not exactly an option. "Our last conversation was strained, to say the least. I walked out on him like I usually do when he pisses me off, and he said something about 'this being the time I regret it'. He was always overdramatic, but then he was murdered that same evening and I can't help but wonder if he knew it was coming."

You're a member of The Assembly for life, and the only way out is exactly what my dad got.

I think about the stories I've heard over the years—people who tried to leave the organization and ended up dead. There was that one man who tried to walk away, only to be found in a car accident that was anything but accidental. Another person, a woman who tried to go public with what she knew, was found dead under mysterious circumstances, her death was ruled a suicide but with too many unanswered questions. And then there was the high-profile case of someone who simply vanished without a trace, leaving behind a chilling reminder of the consequences of crossing The Assembly.

The danger isn't just a vague threat; it's real and tangible, and it feels like a shadow that's always lurking just out of sight.

Jack frowns. "We'll figure it out, baby. I promise. But first, let's get through breakfast, okay? We both need to eat and rest before whatever comes next."

I manage a smile, appreciating the steadiness in his voice. "Okay."

We finish our meal in silence except for Sienna banging her hands against her seat and giggling. Jack keeps a close eye on both of us, his protective instincts seemingly on high alert, the anxious energy in the room evidence that I'm not the only one feeling somewhat at a loss here. It would be nice to know what my dad's people want with *me*, if that's even what's happening here.

There are so many unanswered questions.

So much speculation on my part, and I am certain this will be what drives me insane.

As much as I distanced myself from my parents over the years, apparently it wasn't enough.

After breakfast, we clear the table and wash the dishes together. I can't shake the nagging worry.

"Thank you," I voice from my spot next to him at the sink, hand-drying the last of the plates.

He turns to face me, takes the plate from my hand, and lays it on the counter along with the damp dish towel. "I've got you." He pulls my body flush against his, and I go lax.

I nod. I kind of want to cry.

The sun climbs higher in the sky outside the window, and Sienna squeals from her highchair ready to be released from her confines.

I slowly pull away from him, standing on my tiptoes to place a kiss on the edge of his jaw. I move to walk away, but he pulls me back. Gripping my jaw, he squishes my cheeks together and tilts my face toward his, smacking a kiss on my lips before releasing me. Butterflies take flight in my stomach at the possessive way he handles me; like I've belonged to him all along.

I take Sienna from her seat and carry her tray over to the sink, dropping it inside. She twists her sticky fingers in my hair, but I don't mind. "You need a bath, cutie," I smile down at her.

"I'll grab her a change of clothes." Jack kisses the top of her head and we head up the stairs together.

We make a great team and I can so easily picture us together like this every day.

As we go through the motions of the rest of the morning, I hold onto Jack's promise. No matter what happens next, I feel confident that he meant what he said.

He has me.

I have him too.

IT'S NOT until we've finished putting Sienna down for her nap and I'm curled up on the couch with my laptop catching up on school work before Jack brings up what Stu mentioned last night.

"I'm not sure we can be too careful," he takes a seat next to me, wrapping his arm around my shoulders.

"Careful is my middle name," I say absently, my attention split between what he's saying and the words sprawled across my screen.

"Your middle name is Elise."

I jerk my head toward him and give him a raised eyebrow. "I'm curious exactly how much you know about me that I haven't shared."

He kisses my forehead. "Enough. And I'm about to know more because you're moving in with me." His tone doesn't leave any room for argument.

I close my laptop and toss it to the side.

I struggle to formulate a response. This is insane, but also probably not the worst idea. I'm here most of the time anyway. It's true, moving in so soon feels like jumping off a cliff without checking if there's water below, but the danger of the stalker makes it feel like a necessary risk.

The idea of having this safe place where I don't have to constantly look over my shoulder is incredibly appealing. And if I'm honest, the thought of being here with him is definitely comforting. As much as it terrifies me, the logic starts to outweigh the fear, and I find that it's not hard to convince myself this might actually be the right move.

He uses the crook of his finger to tip my mouth closed, then leans down to kiss me again. I am becoming addicted to the casualness of his touch, and the way his mouth feels on mine.

"Just until we figure this out," he says against my lips before another peck there. "Please?"

I climb onto his lap, straddling him. Maybe forward, but it's not the first time I've been in his lap... or the second. "Where will I sleep?"

I know where *I* want to sleep, and where he *probably* wants me to sleep. I'm mostly teasing.

"I'll have the guest room ready for you by tonight." His eyes sparkle with playfulness.

My mouth falls open again, in mock offense this time, and I pry myself away from him to take my spot on the couch back.

"I'm *kidding*." He closes my laptop again just after I've placed it back on my lap and reopened it.

"Nope," I open it again and smack his hand away. "I prefer to sleep with a fan on, so I would appreciate it if you'd stick one in there after you wash the sheets."

"Quinn."

I ignore him, focusing on my work again. Or at least pretending to.

"*Quinn*."

"You're distracting me." I stand, tossing the blanket I had on my lap back onto the couch. "If you need me, I'll be on the back patio with Kronk."

I start to walk away, but he stands and catches me around the waist, pulling my back against his front and leaving no space between us. "Fine," he bends down and rubs his scruff against my neck. "But the bed in the guest room is *very* uncomfortable."

Pulling away from him this time is an absolute burden, but I commit to the bit. "I could sleep on the tile floor and still sleep like a log, so don't get any ideas about sticking a pea under the mattress to try and wear me down. It won't work." That might have been true at one point in time. The ability to sleep anywhere, unpressed, has always been one of my many talents. Until lately, like pretty much everything else.

He doesn't let me get far before he pulls me into him

again, this time wrapping his fingers around my throat and placing a kiss at the base of my ear that is more tongue than anything. "I plan to have you begging to never leave my bed again by tomorrow night at the latest."

When he releases me I'm a bit breathless. It's kind of embarrassing the effect he has on me. "Counting on it," I say with as much confidence as possible, but I can feel the smugness radiating from him as he watches me walk out of the room and out the back door.

21

PLUS, NO MORE GHOSTIES

QUINN

THE MIDDAY SUN beats down on the campus, and my building looms ominously, a relic from another era with its ivy-clad, cracked stone exterior. The feeling it sparks in my chest is the only reason I feel sad about leaving it behind. I would have moved out in a few months anyway, so it's not like this wasn't inevitable, but the small pang of sadness I feel is there nonetheless. I pull the door open and trudge up the stairs that lead to my dorm, dragging my unfolded packing boxes behind me.

This is likely one of the last times I'll climb these stairs, and while I know how *I* feel about that, Kruz is another story.

She's already waiting by my door when I arrive, and she shivers as we enter the room. Jack was more accepting of me doing this without him because I wouldn't be alone. I insisted he stay with Sienna, and he relented only because his mom already had other plans and he didn't want to fuck with her bedtime routine.

If only he knew that Kruz is an absolute coward who will

run hard and fast in the opposite direction if there's ever a threat to our safety. I'm not sure she wouldn't trip me and leave me for dead just to save herself.

Not that Jack really has a say in what I can and cannot do now, but it is kind of cute when he's bossy in the name of my safety.

I hope he's just as bossy in *other* areas of our relationship too. I suspect he will be. I'll find out soon enough now that I'm shacking up with him for a while, and I am very much looking forward to it.

"Thank god we've finally reached the end of your tenancy here," Kruz crosses her arms over her chest and rubs her hands up and down her biceps as if she can ward off the preternatural chill.

"Thanks for helping," I place a hand on her forearm. Ultimately, it does mean a lot to me that she faces her unfounded fears of the ghost that inhabits my dorm room to help me out whenever I need a hand.

I turn away from her and sigh. Unlocking my door and stepping inside, I chuck the boxes onto my bed. I catch my reflection in the mirror above my desk, my tension headache is evident on my face, and the dark circles under my eyes give away the amount of sleep I got last night.

"Of course," she answers, plopping down on the bed. "No way I'm letting you pack all this up on your own."

I sit down on the floor and start folding the boxes into their proper shapes, carefully creasing the flaps to make sure they hold together well. After a moment, she joins me, settling down beside me with a smile.

Together, we tackle the task, our hands moving in sync as we transform the piles of flat boxes into something usable.

The atmosphere feels lighter with her beside me, and I appreciate the company as we chat about everything and nothing while we fold, both of us avoiding the topic of all the things in my life I wish weren't happening right now. It turns into a surprisingly enjoyable moment, just as every other moment I spend with my best friend.

I should probably not tell her that Jack also claims me as his best friend now too. She'd probably want to kick his ass.

Then again, maybe I would like to see her try that.

Ezra is supposed to drive the moving truck over and help us load it up once we are finished. I'm super curious to see how she reacts to meeting him.

A half an hour later the room is more of a mess than anything, with half-packed boxes and scattered clothes covering nearly every surface. Kruz is folding a pile of shirts, and I am actively trying to ignore the eerie feeling that always seems to hang in the air. It has obviously never bothered me before, but somehow feels more pronounced now that there's an actual threat behind it.

"Are you sure you don't wanna just move in with me?" Kruz asks for the millionth time since I called her and filled her in earlier today. She glances at me while she works. "I mean, moving in with your boss and all. It might be a lot." She gives me a loaded look.

My answer has been the same every time she's asked. Moving into another dorm room mid-semester would be such a hassle, especially with all the paperwork and approvals involved. Kruz had a roommate, but they left after a few weeks, so there's a vacancy, but it's never as simple as just shifting into a new space.

She knows all that's gone on between me and Jack, thanks to our constant stream of texts and nightly phone calls. I tell her everything, even though I knew she'd be smug as fuck with her I-told-you-so attitude.

She's lucky she's cute.

I pause, a stack of books in my arms. "I don't really have a choice," I admit, my voice tinged with anxiety. I try to suppress it for her sake, but at the same time I do want her to know exactly how I am feeling about this.

Besties endure their anxieties together, and I can't protect her from life anymore than I can protect myself from it. It would be unfair for me to not be real with her about this.

"With everything that's been happening... I just can't stay here anymore." I drop the books into a half-filled box. "In the dorms at all, I mean," I add. "It doesn't feel safe, and I especially don't want to drag you into that. Besides, it'll be easier with Sienna and Kronk if I'm there all the time. And the lack of commuting will be nice."

Kruz nods suspiciously, seemingly understanding the words I don't say aloud; that I want to be with Jack too. "This is honestly a nightmare," she groans. The sound is a great representation of how I feel about it. "Maybe the change in scenery will be good for you."

"Yeah," I reply, forcing a smile. "Plus, no more ghosties." I wiggle my fingers.

Kruz snorts. "You know I won't miss that. This place is creepy as hell."

She will probably find Jack's house just as creepy, if not creepier.

I suppress the urge to hum *The Addams Family* theme song out loud and settle for just humming it in my head.

We work in companionable silence for a while, the room slowly emptying as we pack away my lame life. I can't shake the feeling of being watched, but I push it aside, focusing on finishing and getting the hell out of here.

"Remember that time you forced me to try and have a séance in here with you?" Kruz asks, eyeing me with a small amount of contempt. "I've never been so scared in my fucking life."

I laugh at the memory and my mood lightens a smidge because it's one of my favorites. "How could I forget? You nearly jumped out of your skin when the candle flickered."

"That wasn't just a flicker. It was definitely something from the other side," she protests, not seeing the same amusement in the memory as I do.

"Sure, sure," I tease, nodding my head.

"You should be glad I'm even here right now," she says, flipping me off.

I'm more glad than she'll ever know.

"Maybe living in a haunted dorm finally caught up to me." She gives me a flat look, but I smile. It's a genuine, relieved smile. "Here's to new beginnings," I say, raising an imaginary glass.

"A new beginning with a hot dad," she echoes, and honestly she's not wrong.

As we pack the last of the boxes, I can't help but be a little giddy despite everything.

JACK

The sun has already set when the moving truck pulls up the driveway. Ezra offered to help them pack it up and drive it over, which made my life much easier because I didn't have to wake Sienna from her early bedtime once the girls finished packing up.

I'm surprised when he steps down out of the truck and Stu doesn't pop out the other side. He's probably working late. No doubt he'd have been downright giddy to hang around Quinn without me there for an hour or so, if only just to annoy me.

Quinn and Kruz follow closely behind him. I know this is going to be an adjustment for her. My house is vastly different from her dorm. It's much more modern—at least on the inside —with so much open space, and it's larger in every way. While her dorm likely feels cramped and temporary, my place has a sense of permanence that I quietly hope she latches onto.

Not to mention *I'm* here.

It won't be an adjustment for me to have her here all the time, though.

I can't fucking wait to have her in my space 24/7.

I just hope *she* will be happy with the change. It doesn't have to be permanent but I'd be lying to myself and everyone else if I said I didn't want it to be.

Am I getting ahead of myself? Probably.

Do I care? Not really.

"This place is huge," Kruz says as she steps out of her car, slamming the door closed. "What a fucking upgrade from your moldy dorm."

Quinn snort-laughs, getting out of her own vehicle. "Let's hope it lives up to the first impression. I'm sure you'll be spooked in no time."

We start unloading boxes. "I appreciate your help." I pass a heavy box to Ezra.

His typical eremitic demeanor seems to have taken a leave of absence for the evening, and I have a sneaking suspicion why. "My pleasure." His eyes linger on Kruz as she carries an armful of sweaters still on their hangers up the front steps. A smirk plays on his lips before he rushes to open the front door for her.

"Thanks," she replies coolly. I don't know her well or at all, but I suspect this is a side of her she's reserved solely for men she'd like to tell to fuck right off, but can't outright for whatever reason. She steps over the threshold and continues up the stairs without missing a beat, her lack of interest in him is palpable.

Ezra raises an eyebrow, clearly unperturbed. "Not a problem, *morte mea*." He says the words to her retreating form and if she hears him, she doesn't let on.

I give him a dark look.

If he has his sights set on her, there won't be anything I can say or do to deter him, so I leave it. Not that it's any of my business, it's just that she's Quinn's friend, and he's, well... a little obsessive at times.

That's probably an understatement.

His obsessive behavior has driven his success, fueling his

complete dedication to anything he focuses on in both his education and his career.

It doesn't translate as well into personal relationships.

I've tried to reign him in too many times to count, but there are just some things that can't be taught, and the ability to chill the fuck out happens to be one of them.

Quinn passes Kruz on the way back out, the smile on her face heart-stopping. I can't help but wrap my arms around her and plant a kiss on her temple. There's no one here who doesn't know about us, and it won't be a secret from the rest of the world much longer if I have anything to say about it.

She'll be out of my class soon, and there will be nothing standing in the way of our relationship becoming a real, tangible, *public* thing. Wedding bells chime in my mind and god I need to calm the fuck down. *What is wrong with me?*

"Your room okay?" I'm humoring her brattiness for tonight, but this is the last night in my house she'll spend outside of my bed. Still, I'm sure it will be good for her to have her own space here when she needs a little privacy or some time alone.

"Perfect," she smacks a quick kiss on my lips and goes back to unloading.

We continue to dance around one another carrying boxes inside. I can't help but notice Ezra continuously stealing glances at Kruz, who is completely unfazed by his presence.

"So, Kruz," He tries again, his tone nonchalant. "What do you do?"

"I'm a student," she replies curtly, not looking up. It's funny to me that she couldn't give a fuck less about his obvious interest in her. Most women fall all over themselves trying to get his attention. Maybe that's part of her appeal to him; her disinterest.

He's undeterred. "What's your major?"

Kruz finally looks at him, her eyes appraising. "Same as Quinn's."

"Interesting," is all he says to end the conversation.

"I think that's pretty much everything," I say, choosing to ignore whatever this little dynamic is brewing between them.

I have more important things to worry about than my best friend obsessing over Quinn's best friend. However, someone should probably warn her.

Not it.

"Thanks, Jack," Quinn says gratefully, wiping her brow with the back of her forearm. She turns to Kruz, a silent question in her eyes. Kruz nods, giving her friend a reassuring smile.

When the last box is finally placed in Quinn's new room, we breathe a collective sigh of relief.

I clap Ezra on the back and thank him for his help.

He nods, his eyes still glued to Kruz. "Anytime."

Quinn pulls Kruz in for a hug, signaling she's just as ready for them to be gone as I am.

Ezra steps closer to the counter and fiddles with a bottle of sparkling wine that has mysteriously appeared from nowhere. There's a mischievous glint in his eye that tells me I won't be getting rid of him as soon as I'd like. "Up for a drink?" The question is for all of us.

Kruz meets his gaze as she pulls away from Quinn.

"Maybe another time," she says, taking the bottle and making her way around the counter to stick it in the wine fridge, effectively making the decision for all of us. She seems to understand that saying yes would mean overstaying her welcome. I'll have to buy her a thank you present for reading the room. "I'm exhausted."

We say our goodbyes and Quinn walks Kruz out. She's gone before Ezra even makes it back to the truck.

"Thanks again for dealing with that," I dip my head toward the moving truck. I'm standing on the threshold of the door to see him off. Quinn comes back up the steps and sidles her way under my arm as Kruz's headlights disappear out of the driveway.

"Not a problem," he climbs in the truck, waving out the lowered window as he backs down the driveway and into the road.

Quinn rolls her eyes, a smile tugging at her lips. "He's such a flirt. Unfortunately for him, unlike me, Kruz is uninterested in fraternizing with a professor. She's actually extra annoyed because she had her sights set on him to TA for next year and he's all but fallen all over himself for her all evening. Makes things awkward, to say the least."

I snort. "I'll make that abundantly clear to him." I leave out the part where I don't think he'll give a fuck. "But if he catches wind of that, he will likely do everything in his power to make it happen for her."

That's actually an understatement. And it wouldn't be the worst thing for Kruz, because it's pretty uncommon to snag a TA position at the masters level at Cypress.

Ezra *can* remain professional. It's just a matter of whether he will or not.

"Let's get you settled," I say, nudging her into the house and closing and locking the door behind us.

I set the alarm system. I feel a sense of anticipation and I'm not sure if it's anxious dread or excitement or a mix of both.

The next few days will be full of unknowns, but one thing is certain—life is about to get a lot more interesting.

I plan to make the best of whatever that ends up looking like.

22

I SHOULD HAVE BLAMED THE GHOSTS

QUINN

THE GUEST ROOM in Jack's house is straight-up cozy.

Like, *very*.

But the truth is I want nothing more than to exit stage left out of this room and straight into Jack's bedroom. Unfortunately, I am nothing if not a brat, so brat I must.

For tonight anyway.

Kronk is curled up on a massive doggie pillow Jack put on the floor at the foot of the bed. I thoroughly complained to him that I wanted Kronk to sleep in bed with me before kissing him goodnight and kicking him out of my room. I am no match for the giant poof. He is snoring his muffled little doggie snores and I am left to snuggle with my own pillow.

I hope he shreds it at some point in the night.

I toss and turn for several minutes before my mind wanders to how Jack might *help me sleep* if I give in and go crawling back to him and knock on his bedroom door. My mind plays out every sexy scenario of what might happen if I did that, and in no time at all I'm needy and fucking soaked.

Great.

Guess I'll just have to take care of that myself.

I slide my hand slowly down my abdomen, the tips of my fingers brushing across my soft skin, causing chill bumps to rise in their wake. My chest rises and falls with deep breaths, the anticipation of the possibility that Jack could come back at any moment growing.

I reach the band of my silk shorts, hesitating for a moment, savoring the tension. Slipping my hand beneath the fabric and dipping my fingers into the warmth and wetness, I move them in a familiar rhythm, tracing delicate circles that make my back arch involuntarily.

I bite my lip to stifle a moan, my breath quickening and my pussy clenching.

All I can see is Jack, his gorgeous face permanently etched into every corner of my mind. The way his jaw tightens when he's focused, the way his hands look when he runs them through his hair, all of it plays in my head like a loop I can't stop.

I picture his body, the way his dress shirts form fit to his chest, his broad shoulders.

I can feel the phantom weight of him next to me.

Each movement brings a wave of pleasure radiating through my core until I'm completely lost in the sensation, the world outside fading into oblivion.

My orgasm crests and I'm barely falling down the other side when my phone buzzes.

An anxious feeling stabs at my chest until I find the wherewithal to reach over and pick it up to see who the text is from.

Jack: Quinn. The walls are very thin.

Apparently, my lip bite didn't make much of a difference.

Quinn: ...and?

Lying is easier than owning up to masturbating within someone's listening distance, especially when you're masturbating to thoughts of said person.

Jack: I can hear you from my room.

Damn.

Quinn: I don't know what you're talking about. I was asleep and your text woke me up.

I know he won't buy it. I should have blamed the ghosts.

Jack: Well... if you need help "going back to sleep" I'm happy to lend a hand.

I want that.

So bad.

I must not have closed the door to my room all the way because before I can respond, it creaks open, only...

It's not Jack.

And as far as I can see, it's not anyone.

In all the time I spent in my haunted dorm, nothing like this ever happened. Have I left one haunted home for another that's worse?

My heart hammers in my chest when Milo jumps up onto the end of my bed causing me to suck in a breath.

"You stupid fucking cat!" I whisper-scream.

Milo slinks up the bed and settles on my stomach, kneading biscuits into my belly pooch.

Jack: Don't curse your needy pussy. It's not her fault.

My mouth falls open when I realize what he must think

he just heard. I groan, my head falling back against the headboard.

I snatch Milo under his two front legs and pull him up to my face, squishing my cheek against his soft fur, and snapping a selfie in the low light of the room.

I send the picture to Jack as an explanation and hear a bellowed, "What the fuck?!" from the other side of the wall.

I snicker at his jealous reaction and send him another text.

Quinn: Goodnight, Jack.

Kronk is still snoozing away, disturbed by neither Milo's appearance nor the chaotic sounds coming from both me and Jack.

Pathetic dog. *So protective.*

I guess I'm snuggling with the cat tonight.

My screen lights up again with an incoming text.

Jack: Goodnight, baby.

The fact that he is respecting my boundaries is both endearing and infuriating.

I'm looking forward to thoroughly pushing him over the edge tomorrow.

I curl my body around Milo's and close my eyes, quickly falling into a dreamless sleep.

23

THE OBSESSION I HAVE WITH THIS MAN

QUINN

THE WINDOWS in Jack's office are massive—definitely not part of the original architecture. The room itself is charming; dark wood furniture and scattered stacks of papers. It smells like Jack, which makes me want to curl up in his chair and take a nap instead of going to class.

I stand near his desk, cradling Sienna in my arms as she coos and giggles, her tiny fingers grasping at the air. At least it's not my hair this time.

Jack is busy arranging his lecture notes, a look of concentration etched on his face. He's not supposed to be at work today.

"Are you sure about this?" I ask, shifting Sienna to my other hip. "I can always skip class today. It's not a big deal." I would argue that I'm fine on my own, but I'm not sure I am.

He looks up, his blue eyes softening when they meet mine. "I'm not letting you get any further behind than you already are. You need to finish your degree this semester, and you have enough to worry about without adding piled-up schoolwork to the list. You've worked too hard to let some creep disrupt your life." He walks over, gently taking Sienna from me. "Besides, Sienna loves visiting Daddy's office. Right, little bear?"

Sienna giggles, her eyes wide and curious as Jack bounces her. The sight of them together always fills my heart with a warmth I never thought I'd feel again regarding father figures. I love the love he has for her so much it hurts.

"I know, but I hate feeling like a burden," I admit, biting my lip. "You already do so much." Dad of the year and professor extraordinaire, not to mention the new tasks of keeping me sane and alive.

"You're not a burden, Quinn," He says firmly, his expression serious. "You're our Quinny. Our family. We want to be near you. *I* want to be near you."

His words make my heart swell. Family—something I haven't had outside my aunt and Kruz—and hearing Jack say that he considers me such makes me feel valued in a way I haven't felt in such a long time. I nod, taking a deep breath. "Okay. But if anything happens, you'll come get me, right?"

"Promise. I'll be right here, just a phone call away."

I give Sienna a quick kiss on her forehead, inhaling her sweet baby scent, and then turn to leave. The hallways of the college are already buzzing with students, their chatter and laughter a stark contrast to the anxiety that gnaws at my insides. I clutch my bag tightly, scanning the faces around me, wondering if any of them are people I need to be worried about right now.

Jack insisted on driving me to and from classes, but the thought of being watched, of not knowing who could be a part of all this bullshit, has me constantly on edge whether he's around or not.

I wouldn't call the feeling I feel fear. More like annoyance and anger.

I slip into the lecture hall, choosing a seat near the front where I can focus on Professor Scott and, hopefully, remain thoroughly distracted from everything else long enough to absorb what he has to say. Throughout the class, I find my mind wandering back to Jack and Sienna. I picture them in his office, Sienna probably grabbing at his notes while he tries to keep her entertained. A smile tugs at my lips despite the tension in my shoulders.

They keep me sane; most of our time together is filled with pure, unfiltered happiness and it's the best reminder of what really matters in my life.

Despite my best efforts to focus, History of Psychology goes by in a blur and we're excused before I realize how much time has passed.

By the time I gather my things and step out of the classroom, the overcast sky has darkened. The wind picks up, carrying a biting chill that contrasts sharply with the warmth of the lecture hall.

It seems colder outside than it did earlier this morning, the temperature dropping by the hour with the incoming cold snap.

My outfit choice for the day was less than reasonable—a short plaid skirt that does nothing to fight off the chill and a loose-fitting sweater that slides off one shoulder, more revealing than it is warm.

I could've chosen something more practical, but I've still got so many boxes I haven't unpacked, and... I may or may not have picked this outfit to tempt my new roomie. The way the sweater hangs just right, the plaid skirt riding a little higher than necessary—it's all intentional, though I'll never admit that out loud.

I find that I've succeeded in this endeavor when I walk by Jack's window on my way back to his office.

Jack: The length of that skirt is dangerous.

I bite my lip to keep from grinning but fail miserably.

Quinn: Are you creeping on me through your window?

I look up to see if I can see him, but the sun is hitting the window at a weird angle.

Jack: I think you dropped something.

Jack: You should probably turn around and bend over to pick it up.

The obsession I have with this man.

Quinn: I will not be showing the entire student body my lower ass cheeks just so you can sneak a peek, Professor Hollis.

I can't remember a time when I have ever called him anything but Jack, but I'm being playful.

Jack: Such a shame.

Quinn: You're insufferable.

But I really like it.

Jack: I'm obsessed with every inch of you, Miss Ivor.

My heart catches in my throat and I appreciate that he

reciprocates my playfulness. However, what he says next catches me completely off guard.

Jack: Obsessed with the thought of you taking every inch of me.

Heat pools in my lower abdomen. How the fuck am I supposed to respond to that?

QUINN, I FIND, DOES NOT HAVE A GAG REFLEX

JACK

MY MOTHER HAS BEEN GONE with Sienna for less than ten minutes when I see Quinn walk by my office window. She knew Sienna would be staying with Grammy tomorrow for the talk Ezra is giving that she wants to attend, but I wanted to surprise her with an evening alone together.

I always think she looks gorgeous, but she looks particularly irresistible knowing that I will finally have her all to myself for the first time.

I'm leaning against the windowsill and Quinn steps into my office.

The first thing I notice is how the soft fabric of her sweater clings just loosely enough to hint at the curve of her collarbone and the smooth line of her shoulder. The sweater's slipping, revealing a teasing glimpse of skin that draws my gaze to a particularly delicate section of skin and I want nothing more than to carve a small *JH* there with my knife.

She closes the door behind her, her eyes scanning the room.

With a huge effort, I pull my gaze away, stopping my line of thought. I allow the stillness to stretch between us. A concerned look twists her face, making me wonder if somehow she could just tell what I was thinking.

"Where's Sienna?" She closes the distance and I meet her in the middle, wrapping my arms around her midsection and clasping my hands at the small of her back.

"My mom picked her up a little before your class ended."

"I thought she was keeping her tomorrow?"

"She is." I bring my hand up to tuck a loose strand of hair behind her ear.

"I can't believe you didn't let me say goodbye." The look of irritation on her face is adorable.

"I very vividly remember you telling her goodbye a little over an hour ago before you left for class."

She leans into me, inhaling a deep breath and melting against me. "You know what I mean."

I bury my face in her hair, the floral scent of her shampoo filling my nostrils.

She pulls back slightly, her attitude about the situation shifting. "So what I'm hearing is we have the evening to ourselves." Her fingers trace the line of my jaw.

I nod, my hands now resting on her hips. "The whole night and all day tomorrow."

She twists my loose tie around her hand and pulls my face closer to hers. I know that given the situation, we should probably head home, but I feel like I've waited an eternity for this moment and I need her now.

Whatever I can get.

Our eyes meet, the charged silence saying all that it needs

to. I lean into it, capturing her lips in a slow, deliberate kiss—a kiss that promises everything I've been missing out on with her.

She responds eagerly, her hands tangling in my hair as she shoves her tongue down my throat and presses her body against mine.

I groan, pulling back slightly. My breathing is heavy, and I rest my forehead against hers. "*Needy.*" I run my fingers along the hem of her skirt, my knuckles brushing against the bare skin of her thigh. "Wanna bend over for me now that we're in private?" I tease.

I would fuck her right here and now without needing much persuasion, but I would prefer our first time together not to be quick and dirty in my office.

There will be plenty of time for quick and dirty later.

She freezes but shakes it off quickly and gives me a suggestive smile. "I have other things in mind."

When she palms my cock through my pants, it's completely unexpected and my hips jerk involuntarily. I grip the back of her neck and kiss her again, our mouths melding perfectly. "And what are those things?" I ask against her lips.

"I have a list."

"I like the sound of that," I say between kisses. "What's on this list?"

She loosens my tie further and removes it from my neck. Even in the short time it takes her to do so, my lips ache to be against hers again. I want to consume every part of her.

Cognizant of the fact that there is a possibility we could be being watched at any given moment, I nudge her to walk backward to the alcove in the corner of my office. Now that we're out of the view of the window, I feel more inclined to do whatever it is that she asks of me.

My office is on the second floor, but I feel extra paranoid about everything right now regarding Quinn. The need I have to make sure this all works out for the best for her—for *us*—is real. I know there is likely a threat to my job because fraternizing with students is definitely against the rules, and I'm about to fuck one of mine in my office.

Her face, anyway.

I just hope she cares as little about that happening as I do because if I have to choose between my job and her, I will gladly take up crochet and sell baby blankets on Etsy for a living.

"Number one," she stands on her tiptoes, kissing down the length of my neck and wrapping the tie around the back of it. It drapes limply over my shoulders. "Teach me how you like your cock sucked, *Professor*."

She drops to her knees before I can respond, and my mouth hangs open while my brain tries to play catchup. We just went from zero to sixty, and I don't even know if my office door is locked.

I also don't even know if I care. I honestly wouldn't under normal circumstances, but I have to think about Quinn.

However, I can't think about anything when she takes my belt off and undoes the button and zipper on my pants.

She takes my cock out and runs her tongue along the underside of it. "Like this?"

I can't form words.

She laps at the precum beading at the top. "*Like this,* Professor?"

I twist her long dark hair around my fist and pull her head back, forcing her to look up at me. Until now, our relationship has been slow and sweet. I haven't minded. We have both been tentative given the nature of our situation, but I need to make it clear to her that I will be anything but *sweet* when given the opportunity to use her body how I've wanted to from the moment she fell into my lap.

With a small amount of space between us, I close my eyes and suck in a breath, steadying myself. I run my free hand over the back of my neck and feel my tie there. She took it off for a reason, and I hope it's the same reason I have in mind now.

I tug at it, allowing the loose end to fall to the floor.

Finally, I look down at her. She hasn't taken those pretty green eyes from my face, and the look in them nearly undoes my composure.

Not that I had much left to begin with when it comes to her.

I shift around her, the head of my cock grazing her jawline as I do. Dropping onto my knees behind her, I band my forearm around her waist, pulling her against me.

"You want me to teach you how I like my cock sucked, Quinn?" I whisper the words hot against her ear.

She nods her head enthusiastically.

"Words, baby."

"Yes," she spits out.

"You're going to be such a fast learner, aren't you, Miss Ivor?" I am under no delusions that she needs me to teach her anything. This is nothing more than a little light role-play, the use of our respective honorifics evidence of that.

But I'm willing to humor her—to lean into this dynamic so I can use it to show her this side of me.

"Yes," she says again.

A quick learner, indeed.

I twist the length of silk fabric around her small wrists, just tight enough that she can feel the restraint of it, but not so tight that she can't remove it herself if she wants or needs to.

"This okay?" I whisper, tugging gently at the material. I don't want to go any further without checking in with her first. Just because I assume this is what she insinuated that she wanted doesn't mean I should take that at face value without asking her to voice it aloud.

"More than," she replies, and I am not sure my cock has ever been harder than it is at this moment.

I hinge at the hips, angling my face to place a kiss at the edge of her jaw. "That's my good girl."

She squirms at my praise, and I like it a lot.

"I like my cock sucked, *Miss Ivor*," I say her name like a taunt. "By you, bound at my feet, loving the way I fuck your face so much that you'll be thinking about the feel of me down your pretty throat for days."

I stand again and move back in front of her. She looks up at me—waiting for my instruction—with such trust that I almost blow my load on her face right then and there.

I try to imagine the most unattractive thing I can think of to prolong this. Decomposing flesh comes to mind.

That does the trick.

I tap beneath her chin wordlessly as I stroke my shaft. She opens for me so fucking obediently. There is a look on her face I've seen plenty of times, but not one I want to see in this scenario.

She's nervous.

I pause. "You okay?"

She nods, opening her mouth and sticking out her flattened tongue, but the anxious look in her eyes is still there.

I have wanted her from the moment I laid eyes on her, but I will never be so lost in the need I feel that her comfort won't be my number one priority. "What happened to those words you were so good at a few minutes ago, baby? Talk to me." My cock throbs painfully.

She closes her mouth, then opens it again, this time trying to find words. "I've never done this before."

Oh.

She literally wants me to teach her.

Is she a virgin? I don't ask the question even though it's the first thing that pops into my mind. I am definitely not fucking her until we talk about this, though. Not because I think virginity is some precious thing a woman chooses to give away, but because I want to be sure I'm caring for her physical needs to the best of my ability.

She's probably not, but you never know.

"Why don't we wait until—"

"No," she cuts me off. "I don't want to wait," she says, softer. "Yeah, I'm nervous because this is new to me. But that does not mean I am not also very excited and eager."

To make her point she opens her mouth again, waiting, as if that's that.

I mean, I guess it is.

Except, she needs to be the one in control here.

For now.

I rest the head of my cock on her tongue and she closes her lips around it. I shudder. "Suck, baby. Take as much as you can. There's nothing you can do that won't feel amazing."

Quinn, I find, does not have a gag reflex.

She bobs her head once and takes me to the back of her throat. My fingers thread in her hair again, this time tightening at her roots because I need her to slow the fuck down.

I was not expecting that.

I want to ask her if she practiced on a banana or something because *what the fuck?*

She follows my lead, popping off me and my cock smacks against my lower abdomen.

"What happened to you fucking my face, *Professor?*" She challenges me.

A low growl builds in my throat. She can be so bratty at times and I like it a fucking lot.

"Oh, I will," I yank her head back a fraction. "But first I want you to untie your hands and slip those pretty little fingers under your skirt. I want to hear how soaked you are." I'm not coming without her, that's for damn sure.

She does as I ask, her nerves seeming to have eased now that everything's out in the open.

I don't think her sexual history is anything she should feel obligated to share with me, but if it makes her feel better for me to know, I'm happy to hear whatever she wants to tell me.

She snakes her hand under the hem of her skirt, and there is a small feral part of me that wants to say fuck this; jerk it away, and toss her on the couch. Eat her pussy until she's screaming so loud the people in the offices surrounding mine call campus security for a wellness check.

She wraps her free hand around the base of my cock, taking me into her mouth again and making the decision for me.

All of the anxiousness and tentativeness from before is gone.

Quinn is an amazing multitasker, sucking my soul from my cock while she works to bring herself over the edge.

I'm close—so fucking close—way sooner than I anticipated, and it has everything to do with how perfect she is.

A whispered *fuck* slips from my mouth.

I don't know that there's anything she could ask of me that I wouldn't do for her.

She groans around my shaft and I make good on my promise, gripping the back of her neck and fucking her face so she can focus on the movements of her hand between her thighs.

Our bodies tighten and snap simultaneously, so suddenly that I forget to ask if she's okay with me spilling down her throat.

It's too late now.

Release barrels down my spine, my balls tightening and emptying with a force that almost brings me to my knees.

Once we're both spent, I *do* fall to my knees, wrapping my arms tight around her.

I bite back the urge to apologize for blowing in her mouth without asking.

She kisses the side of my neck, nipping at my earlobe

once she reaches it. "I don't know what I expected, but it wasn't that."

I stiffen at her words and pull back, tilting her face toward mine. Maybe that was too much for her first time. "Quinn, I'm sorr—"

"That was amazing." She buries her head at the base of my throat and I breathe in her scent.

I think I could die happy at this moment because the woman I'm rapidly falling for is perfect in every way.

I can't wait to get her home and into my bed.

25

I WANT TO SEE THESE BOUNCE

QUINN

THE EVENING AIR is cool and crisp as I follow Jack down the narrow path that twists around the side of his house leading to the backyard. We find Kronk there, who loses his fucking mind when he spots us.

The feel of Jack still lingers in the back of my throat, and I can't get enough of the feeling or the taste of him on my tongue. Who knew someone who has always been mostly attracted to women would enjoy sucking cock so fucking much?

Not me, that's for sure.

But I'm excited to do it again.

And soon.

Jack unlocks the back door, pushing it open with a creak. Kronk's nails tippy tap across the hardwood floor as he bolts to the laundry room breaking the silence that's settled over the house.

"After you," he gestures for me to enter before him. I grin, stepping inside and trailing after Kronk to give him his bedtime snack and fill his inside water bowl. I'm glad he loves his crate so much that this is the first place he comes when we let him back inside, but I still feel kind of bad leaving him in here all night now that he's gotten used to sleeping upstairs most nights.

I don't linger on it. I plan on thoroughly focusing on Jack tonight. Kronk will be just fine.

I lock his crate and close the laundry room door, silencing the sounds of him lapping up his water.

Back in the main area of the house, Jack is nowhere to be found.

I climb the stairs and pad down the hallway, following the sound of running water coming from his cracked bedroom door.

When I enter the room, I hear him in his bathroom brushing his teeth.

I make myself comfortable on his bed. I don't know if it's physical exhaustion or mental that pulls me under, but the sounds of him cleaning up for the night lull me to sleep before he ever comes out of the bathroom to join me.

When I peel my eyes open what feels like hours later, Jack has crawled into bed with me, not bothering to wake me.

It makes my heart pinch at the fact he let me sleep when I know he had other plans in mind.

My body itches at how close we are to one another. The distance between us feels weighty, brimming with intense longing. His thick thigh is barely an inch from my fingertips, and I curl my hand into a fist to stop myself from touching him.

I know it's inevitable.

We are going to fuck.

If not now, eventually, and probably soon.

But if he let me sleep, I should do the same for him.

Or...

His sheets are draped low on his hips, revealing a glimpse of the boxers he's wearing underneath.

I undress quickly, leaving only my lacy panties on, and climb back onto the bed. With a gentle tug, I pull the sheet off of him to straddle his body.

He doesn't wake, but I can't resist aligning our bodies so perfectly that if he were awake and hard, we would fit together seamlessly.

My pussy flutters at the thought, and I grind my clit against his thick length almost involuntarily.

The only part of him that stirs is his cock, and the feeling of him twitching against my core spurs me on.

I lean down, kissing him softly on the lips. His breathing deepens, and he shifts in his sleep.

I grin, hoping that he loves waking up like this because I would love to make a habit of it. My heart races in anticipation as I lean in further, teasing him with soft, wet kisses against his neck.

Each touch brings him closer to consciousness, and I savor every moment. With a final peck on his full lips, I pull back slightly, trailing my hand down his naked chest, feeling the strength of his muscles beneath my fingertips.

I grind my body against his, his breath hitching as my movements become more urgent.

My own pleasure builds with each jerk of my hips, but he

continues to sleep despite his thickening cock, unaware that I'm about to come completely undone on top of him.

Unaware that I'm using his body like a little slut.

My hands dance across his skin, moving up to cup his face. I lean down closer to him as my body tenses with an orgasm.

The tendrils of consciousness weave themselves into his brain, and he responds to me with a gasp as he fully wakes.

He looks into my eyes, a mixture of surprise and desire reflecting there. His hands move to grip my hips, holding me flush against him as my body convulses in pleasure.

His hand slides up my back, stopping between my shoulder blades and splaying there as I regain my bearings.

"Couldn't wait for me to wake up, baby?" he asks in a gentle, teasing voice, hoarse from sleep. He calls me baby so often now, and it's so fucking sweet it makes my teeth ache.

I sit up, my face flushing now that he's cognizant of the fact that I just fucked myself to orgasm on his half-hard dick while he slept.

It's fully hard now, so apparently he doesn't mind.

His gaze remains on me, as intense as ever. I'm often thankful he seems to say whatever's on his mind because otherwise, he is unreadable.

I take in every detail of his face—the sharpness of his jawline, the permanent dimple cratering his cheek, and his pouty lips, slightly damp from running his tongue across the seam.

My eyes track the movement and I shift my body, too antsy, when I think about how I know what they taste like.

How I want to taste them again.

And so much more.

We are on the same wavelength. Only, he is less hesitant than I am because he has no reason to feel the embarrassment I currently feel about what I just did.

He pulls my face to his again. Our lips hover a breath apart, and then he closes the distance. It's a light, almost tentative brush, different from all the other times we've crossed this line.

He can't seem to hold back any longer, and I don't want him to.

I press my lips harder against his.

He responds with an equal hunger and urgency, very similar to the first time he kissed me. Our bodies press together and I can feel every inch of him.

Something inside me screams *more*.

His hands find their way to my hips. Mine travels up to tangle in his thick hair, another trailing over the defined muscles of his chest. We move in sync, our touches growing more frenzied with each passing second. I whimper into his mouth as he pulls me closer, my sensitive core grinding against his hard cock as if I could take any more of that right now.

He sits up, lifting me and shifting our bodies. My back hits the bed and he covers every inch of me with every inch of him, pressing his thick shaft against my pussy and grinding himself against me as he assaults me with heated kisses.

"This. You. It's all I want," I whisper against his wet lips.

He moves to my neck and trails his hot mouth to my collarbone.

His fingers roam along my rib cage and trace all too

fucking lightly around my pebbled nipple. "Tell me," his gaze is heated, hungry. *Starving.* "How much?" His breath tickles my ear as he whispers, "Gonna make you moan it for me."

"You're so perfect," I say between kisses. I can't resist nipping at his lip, and he's the one who moans.

His eyes are half-lidded as he reaches for my waistband. I eagerly yank at his boxers and he shifts to slide them down and we strip off what little we are wearing, our limbs entwined and bodies moving against each other.

He slides the head of his cock along my drenched seam. "You *do* want me," he smirks.

I appreciate his perpetual playfulness. It briefly takes my mind off the fact I've never done this before. I mean, I have. Had sex, that is. Just not with a man. I'm not a virgin by any means. I feel like I should say all of this out loud to him. He doesn't need to know my entire sexual history, nor do I need to know his, but it feels important, this admission. *Perhaps that is because of the stigma society has placed on the concept of virginity*, I think, and decide that now is not the time for that conversation.

It would ruin the mood. It's not as if his dick will be the first thing that's ever been inside of me. Just the first non-silicone *dick*. I mean, it may be a tight fit, but there definitely won't be any other inclination of virginity on my part.

I have *got* to get out of my own head. I want to enjoy this. "Stop teasing me," I huff back, equally as playful, though maybe a bit forced.

His fingers wrap around his length, stroking it in a teasing manner.

As if he could make it any harder.

The jerky movement of his hand makes me feel like I might burst, but he doesn't make me wait any longer. He glides the tip over my throbbing clit, causing my body to jerk before he eases inside my aching core.

His large hands grasp my thighs roughly, parting them to give himself a better angle—and a better view.

He is slow, teasing, entering me only halfway before pulling back out again. His thick cock glistens with my arousal as he slides in deeper this time, stretching me in a way I've never been stretched before. The groan that escapes me is not human.

It is a tight fit, and the pressure and burn of it is far more than I expected.

I am breathless, *full*.

I want to spend every day for the rest of forever full of Jack Hollis.

He maintains his slow pace, his need for me is barely contained and written all over his face. My body writhes beneath him, and I thrust myself upward.

He grips my hip and pins me to the mattress, closing his eyes as he stills his movements and sucks in a breath. "Don't move."

I want to move. Watch him lose control. Send him straight off the deep end.

He regathers his composure and readjusts us both, hooking my bent knee over his own. His next thrust is unbearably deep, and hard in a way that makes me feel like I might come out of my fucking skin.

"Oh fuck!" The words are louder than I intend.

He cants his hips slower, more deliberately, but just as rough. "There?" He asks, rutting into me. I nod my head fervently, my skin flaming. "That's *oh fuck?*"

He tilts his pelvis, grinding the head of his cock against a spot inside me I didn't know existed before now, and my pussy clenches and flutters around his length.

"*Fuck,*" he breathes. "I could live here. I want to fucking live here."

He holds himself there for a moment before pulling out almost completely and then driving back into me faster and harder than before. I cling to the bedsheets, overwhelmed by all of him in every way.

He slows his pace again. His rough fingers lightly brush over my sensitive nipple and I arch into his touch.

Without warning, he stops and withdraws from me. "Ride me," he says like he's just thought of something life changing and he lays down on the bed next to me. "I want to see these bounce," he palms my breasts as I move to straddle him again.

I obey his command, straddling him as his firm grip takes hold of my waist, guiding me onto his body.

I eagerly take him inside again, thankful for how wet he makes me because *oh my god it's a lot*. Leaning forward, my hands grip the contours of his muscled chest as I begin to ride him with increased speed and intensity. My breasts bounce with each movement and Jack's hand finds its way to cup one of them. He kneads my flesh, causing blissful sparks to shoot through my body.

"I wish I could keep you like this day and night," he groans, his voice filled with awe. "You ride dick so good, baby." The sound of skin slapping against skin echoes in the room and I can't help but let out a loud moan as my body is overcome by waves of pleasure.

"Me too," I murmur as his hands grip my waist. Another wave of heat rushes over my skin. My legs quiver slightly as he guides me, his movements precise. "Oh god," I gasp, my orgasm building from the way he grinds my clit against his pelvis. "I'm going to come."

He gradually slows the way he fucks up into me even though I am supposed to be the one riding him, and I match his pace, savoring his deep and deliberate thrusts that send waves of pleasure through my body. With a steady rhythm, I move up and down on his cock, each motion pushing me closer to the edge.

He is everything and I never want this to end.

"Don't you dare fucking stop," he growls, his voice laced with urgency.

My muscles burn with fatigue, but I push myself to keep going at this feverish pace. I watch as his face contorts in pleasure, his eyes glazing over. He lets out a low, guttural moan that travels down my spine. Every nerve in my body is on fire.

The most intense orgasm of my life wracks my entire being as my body convulses in pleasure. At the same time, Jack reaches his own peak and we both come to a shuddering halt, completely spent and sated in each other's embrace.

I fall over into a heap on his slick body. "I've never," I say, curling against him.

"Me neither," he breathes, brushing my hair from both our faces.

I know he doesn't mean that in the same way I do, but in

a way I think we are on the same page. Because while I mean physically, I also mean emotionally.

You're the first, I don't say aloud. *The first person I think I might be in love with too.*

26

NEED SOMETHING?

JACK

IT WAS a nice thought that we would wake up the following day—after fucking through every hour of the night—and attend a lecture together, but that isn't what happened.

Quinn is in the backseat with Sienna, who is safely strapped into her car seat and snoozing away despite how horrible she must feel. Meanwhile, I drive in a dazed and exhausted state as we approach the driveway.

The high from last night evaporated quickly when Grammy video called early this morning, Sienna's face appearing on the screen flushed from puking her poor baby guts out.

Once I put the car in park, Quinn takes her out of her car seat, attempting to soothe her back to sleep. I open the door and she hands her off to me so I can carry her inside and upstairs. Worry strains my brow and I can feel a tension headache from hell coming on.

"I hope she doesn't have a fever." This is the first time

she's been sick, something I've dreaded since the day I brought her home fresh out of the hospital.

Quinn nods, setting up my bedroom for a long night ahead. She pads into the bathroom and wets a washcloth.

As we settle, so does my initial panic. I run the cool cloth over my little bear's forehead. Quinn, who is the picture of calm, focuses on ordering an electrolyte drink and other groceries to be delivered. "She's going to be okay," she reassures me softly, "Babies get sick. I'm sure she just picked up a bug somewhere."

I nod. Logically, I know. But at the same time, I am also contemplating if I could stick her inside of some kind of antiviral bubble for the rest of her childhood. "I just hate seeing her like this. Do you think we should take her to the doctor?"

"Let's wait a few hours before we risk exposing her to more germs," she suggests, her voice soothing. "Usually there's not much that needs to be done for a stomach bug as long as we keep her hydrated."

Less than an hour later Sienna's breathing evens out and her eyelids flutter as she drifts back to sleep. I plop down in the chair next to her crib and take in a deep breath. Quinn's eyes are fixed on me. I can tell she's worried because I'm worried and I feel a pang of guilt for stressing her.

"Why don't you come lay down?" She pats the bed next to where she's sitting. "I'll stay up with her."

I shake my head. "I don't think I could sleep even if I tried."

"Wanna watch Nightmare Before Christmas?" A playful smirk tugs at the corner of her mouth and I pop up out of the chair so fucking fast, my body pulled toward hers like it's being controlled by some unknown force.

"*No*," I say, all but tackling her, laying us both down on the bed and tugging her against my chest. She wraps her arm around me and curls her body against mine.

Sienna has watched the movie on repeat for days now and if I have to hear Jack Skellington sing, "What's this?" even one more time, my head might explode. I realize she's too young for very much screen time, but it's mostly on as background noise. She loves it when we sing along to the songs, and initially, I thought it had to be better than Cocomelon. Turns out that if you play anything on repeat enough times, it can send a person into psychosis.

"Got any better ideas?" She giggles.

Oh, I have lots of ideas for things we could do aside from sleep.

None of them are appropriate to participate in with a sleeping baby in the room.

That's why I climb out of bed and scoop Quinn up, carrying her bridal style to the bathroom. She stifles a giggle as the door quietly snicks shut.

Gently, I lower her back onto her feet and reach into the shower to turn on the water. I take the liberty of slowly removing her clothes before shedding my own.

The sound of the water hitting the tiles blends with our hurried breaths as we become lost in each other's touch. The air is thick with steam and heat when I pull her under the spray.

As badly as I want to fuck her into the tile, the truth of the matter is that neither of us had time to shower this morning because we left in such a hurry. There's nothing I want more than to just take care of her right now.

I take my time, gently working the shampoo into her long, thick hair. Suds glide down her back and shoulders as I massage her scalp. Once the last traces of conditioner have been rinsed away, I move on to the rest of her, gently stroking every inch of her skin with my soapy hands.

Fuck using a loofah, I want my skin on hers.

Every dip and curve on her body is a fucking work of art, and the urge I have to mark it as my own is all-consuming at this moment.

She sighs as I curl my hand around the crease of her thigh, my thick cock hard against the middle of her back. Her head falls back against my chest and I love that she goes so limp in my arms.

While I plan to give her several, the fact that she is already so relaxed with me without having even been given an orgasm? Everything.

Her hips undulate like they have a mind of their own, and I flatten my hand against the lowest part of her stomach, forcing her body flush against mine.

"Need something?" I tease her, but it's unfounded. However much she needs me, I need her tenfold. Maybe more.

She grinds herself roughly against my erection. "Do you?"

"Yeah, I fucking do."

I flip our positions and push her against the cool tile of the shower. Her back arches as she lets out a gasp, surprised and turned on by the rough way I handle her.

Dropping to my knees, I hook one of her legs over my shoulder and lap at her pussy like it's the best thing I've ever tasted. I think it might be.

It's addicting if nothing else.

She squirms and tries to muffle her moans, but I can feel the tension building in her body. Too quickly, she succumbs to the pleasure, soaking my face.

Every part of my being is focused on pleasuring her, making sure she feels every sensation possible, so even after she comes down from her orgasm, I can't find it within myself to stop.

As she weakly attempts to push me away, I suck her clit between my lips, and shove two fingers inside her drenched pussy, fucking her with my hand and mouth until she is overcome with another wave of ecstasy.

She rides the wave, shuddering and clenching around my fingers. I press my lips against her hip bone, and when she dips her head to gaze down at me, I am sure that there will never be a better feeling than the one I feel when I make her look at me like this.

I stand, sliding my body against hers as I do. She wraps her arms around my neck and all but climbs me like a tree once I'm fully upright, kissing me with such urgency that it feels like she needs my lips on hers more than oxygen itself. I can feel her moans vibrating through my entire body, and it sends a shudder down my spine. I almost come from the sound alone.

"You like the taste of yourself, baby?" I murmur between kisses. "So good, huh?"

She nods and dives back in. Water beats over our faces.

I'm suffocating. Drowning.

I can think of worse ways to go.

She grinds against me, needy to be filled and I like it so much I consider making her writhe and beg a little longer despite the fact my cock is so hard it's fucking painful.

I impale her on my thick length, holding her in place as I take a minute to breathe through the pleasure of it. She feels so fucking good it should be illegal, and it's hard to last very long without giving it a solid effort.

For a split second, my mind flits to the fact that Sienna could wake up from her nap at any time. *Dad life*; thinking of your baby every waking moment, even the most inopportune ones.

With that fleeting thought, I chase my release, pounding into her relentlessly because I desperately do not want to be interrupted before I fill her up.

My release comes hard and fast and I press her back into the wall and rest my face against her wet shoulder.

In my hazy comedown, I realize we haven't had the birth control discussion and I feel like a dipshit for not even asking if it was okay for me to finish inside her any of the times that I have now.

I don't expect that someone preparing to go into their master's program would be eager to get knocked up, and she's well aware that I already have the responsibility of *one* baby.

I think we're good, but I make a mental note to bring it up to her at a later date.

A date in which I'm not currently inside of her, my cum already dripping down the insides of her thighs.

There is a feral part of me that whispers; *it wouldn't be so bad, would it? Another baby? With her?*

Yeah, this woman has me losing my fucking mind. What the hell is wrong with me?

I lower her onto the slick tile floor, my face scrunching with a smile as her bare feet slap against the surface. As she presses a soft kiss against my chest, Sienna wails from the other room signaling she's awake.

"What timing," I half snort, half laugh.

"I'll grab her," she stands on her tiptoes to kiss the corner of my mouth. "You finish up."

"Thanks, baby." I appreciate the offer being that I haven't *actually* showered.

She steps out and wraps up in a towel before padding into the bedroom to grab Sienna.

I can hear them through the cracked door. She shifts so easily back into mom mode, and my heart pinches a little because that's what it is, isn't it? She's mothering my child and it's a huge part of why I think I'm falling in love with her.

Every day, she becomes more of the missing puzzle piece that we didn't even know was missing. She fills the role so effortlessly as if it was always meant to be hers.

God, I hope that what I have to offer in return is enough to make her want to stay.

27

MIMOSA DOES NOT TASTE AS GOOD THE SECOND TIME AROUND

QUINN

I COME BACK INSIDE from taking Kronk out, put on a pot of coffee, and pull out the things I need to make breakfast. Yesterday was thoroughly exhausting, but Sienna felt better by the evening and was seemingly back to normal by last night.

We spent the entire day snuggling in bed and—to Jack's dismay—watching *The Nightmare Before Christmas*.

I did get another call from the station about another arrest having been made, and neither of us has gotten any more creepy texts, so now I'm wondering if there's no one left for us to have to worry about.

My loves are still snoozing, and I feel a rare sense of calm as I crack eggs into a bowl and whisk them into a frothy mixture, the quiet, early-morning silence giving me a moment to rewire my brain.

In an attempt to lift everyone's spirits this morning, or at least mine, I make my way over to the wine fridge and grab a bottle of prosecco. With a satisfying pop, I uncork it and pour myself a mimosa, loving the mix of citrus and breakfast smells. Each sip makes me more optimistic about the day ahead.

Humming to myself as I finish setting the table, Jack comes down the stairs. My heart skips a beat at the sight of him in his messy-haired glory.

"Morning," he greets me with a kiss. "What's all this?"

I grin up at him. "Just thought I'd spoil my two favorite people with a yummy brekkie. How's Sienna?"

"She's still sleeping, but I suspect that once her batteries are fully recharged, we're both in for it."

He's probably right. She has lost time to make up for. I pour and hand him a mimosa, thinking we're both going to need it for entirely different reasons once baby girl wakes up.

He clinks his glass against mine and places it on the countertop without taking a drink before stepping over to pour himself a cup of coffee. "Can't wreck my freshly brushed teeth with OJ."

I'm plating our omelets when a sudden sharp pain hits my stomach. Sucking in a breath, I manage to place them down before I double over.

"You okay?" Jack is by my side in an instant.

I nod, but the pain only gets worse along with a wave of nausea. Struggling to stand, I barely make it to the sink before puking my guts out. Mimosa does *not* taste as good the second time around.

Once I recover, I turn on the water to rinse the puke down the drain and cringe to myself that I just upchucked in front of him. "I think I might have Sienna's bug."

Way to state the obvious, Quinnifer.

He rubs the small of my back. His phone buzzes in his pocket. He ignores it, focused on me until it buzzes again.

And again.

He furrows his brow, confused. I'm wondering the same thing—who could be texting him so insistently? With a sigh, he pulls the phone out and taps the screen. His expression shifts from confusion to pure shock.

"What is it?" Worry coils in my stomach, even though there's already more than enough to deal with. I dry heave over the sink again, nausea gripping me.

He absently uses his free hand to gather my hair into a loose ponytail, holding it back as I wretch. "It's my sister." His voice is tight as he places his phone on the counter, turning toward me. "She overdosed. They just took her to the hospital."

The weight of his words hangs in the air. My heart aches for him, but all I can manage is a strained, "Is she... okay?"

I see something like hope in his eyes, fragile and fleeting, an unspoken wish that all of this ends up being fine—that maybe this will be her wake up call. An ache forms deep within my chest. I want to be hopeful for him, but there's a part of me that recoils at the thought. That little girl inside me, the one who used to hope her parents would choose her for once, is clawing her way to the surface when I think of all the times Jack's sister has not chosen her daughter.

It's hard to be hopeful for someone else's situation when hope has only ever brought me disappointment.

It's hard to be hopeful when the outcome of this could be so much worse than any of that.

"I don't know. I feel like I have to go. But I—" He hesitates, his voice cracking, his hand still resting on my back. "I can't just leave you here like this." I know he doesn't just mean because I am sick, but because of everything else too.

"You have to go," I say, swallowing the nausea rising in my throat. "I'll be fine. It's just a stomach bug. You need to be there for her."

"I don't know how long it'll take... It's three hours one way. What if—" He shakes his head, the uncertainty and worry clear on his face.

"I'll be safe here," I assure him, forcing a weak smile. "The security system's on, and our three besties are just a phone call away. Go. You need to be with her."

He scrubs his hands over his face, clearly torn, before pulling me into his arms. "I don't know what's right, but I feel like I have to." His words are strained.

I rub his back gently, trying to comfort him even though I feel like I'm barely holding on myself. "It's hard when you don't have time to think about it, but you know what you have to do. If you are worried about me being here alone, we can call Kruz or one of the guys to come over for a while."

His grip on me tightens before he pulls away slightly, resting his forehead against mine. "You're right. But I hate leaving you like this."

"I'll pack a bag for Sienna while you get ready," I offer, even though I already feel the energy draining from me. "You should eat something before you go."

"*You* will do no such thing." He gently lifts me off my feet as if I weigh nothing at all and carries me toward the stairs. "I'm putting you back to bed and we'll come say our goodbyes once we're ready to head out."

I want to grumble something back at him, but the energy I had when I woke up this morning is fading fast, so I just wrap my arms around his neck, rest my head on his shoulder, and enjoy the ride to his bedroom.

He's tucking me back into his bed when Sienna decides to wake up.

She squeals as he lifts her from her crib. "Somebody's feeling much better today," he says, peppering her fat cheeks with kisses.

"Daddy's not gonna be feeling too hot himself if he doesn't stop getting up close and personal with his girls while they're still germy," I note, sinking further into the pillows and curling up in his comforter. It smells like him and honestly, I could just live here from now on, thanks.

"I fear my impending doom is inevitable." He props Sienna on his hip. She reaches for me, grunting as she tries to jerk herself out of his arms. "Quinny is sick, you little petri dish," he tells her.

"Give her to me and go make a bottle. I'll feed her while you shower. We can watch Oogie." I take the remote from his nightstand and flick on the TV.

Jack goes through the motions of changing her and dressing her for the day before handing her over, he is seemingly feeling pretty normal but I can't help but feel anxious for him knowing the emotions that are likely warring inside him right now. He is very good at masking how he feels when it comes to not wanting to burden me with extra worry, it seems.

Thankfully I don't puke again.

A little over an hour later, Sienna is fed and thoroughly

Oogied out. Jack has showered, dressed, and arranged for his mom to keep Sienna for the day. She was more than happy to have her back, especially since she hadn't wanted us to take her in the first place, even with her being sick, but neither of us felt good about being away from her while she felt bad.

"Are you sure you'll be okay while I'm gone?" Jack asks me for what feels like the millionth time.

"Positive," I say, squeezing Sienna one last time before he snatches her up off the bed and places a chaste kiss on my forehead. "I'll miss you both, though."

"We'll be back tonight, and I'll text you updates." He brushes his thumb along my cheek, hesitating like he can't bear to leave me.

He really is everything. How did I get here?

"I'll have necessities delivered," he adds, sitting down on the edge of the bed to give me one last group hug. "Please make sure you try and eat something in a few hours."

"I will." I snuggle them both close and Sienna smacks a drooly kiss on my cheek at the same time Jack kisses my temple. "I love you two." The words tumble out before I realize what I'm saying, and I want nothing more than the ability to shovel them back into my mouth and swallow them whole.

I *do* love them, but it's probably way too soon for me to be saying that to Jack.

He pulls back, seemingly shocked, and rightly so. Sienna is completely oblivious to the fact that I just made everything suuuuuper awkward.

Except, when he grasps my chin and runs his thumb along my jawline, staring at me like he's trying to formulate an apt response, I realize that maybe I'm *not* fully eating my shoe right now.

"We love you, too," he says. "*I* love you."

They're gone for over an hour before I come down from the high of that admission, and only then it's because the doorbell rings, jerking me out of my lovesick stupor.

28

DECOMPOSE WITH THE OTHER SKELETONS DOWN THERE

QUINN

I'M LESS sick than I anticipated, but still feel like I have sludge in my veins when I drag myself downstairs to answer the door.

I'm surprised to find Stu waiting on the other side. "Jack texted," he frowns, looking me over and holding up a bag stuffed to the brim with various items. "I brought stomach virus necessities."

I step out of the way and he slips by me, giving me a wide berth.

"Ugh, thank you. Just sit it on the island." I cross my arms over my chest and lean against the closed door. I expect him to bolt, but he starts unloading the contents of the bag. "You don't have to stick around, I'm not that sick."

He waves me off and continues what he's doing. "It's fine. Have you tried to eat anything yet?" He shakes a container of what looks like egg drop soup, and I all but drool. Why is it the best thing ever for every illness?

I cringe. "No. I'm not sure I can yet."

He turns and opens a cabinet and pulls out a bowl. "Well, you should at least try." He jerks his head toward the living room. "Go sit down, I'll heat this up and bring it to you."

I hesitate for only a moment before doing as he asks. Jack genuinely has some of the best friends.

I left my phone on the nightstand, but don't have the energy to climb the stairs again to grab it. "Hey," I yell to the kitchen. "Could you text Jack to check on things? I left my phone upstairs."

His face appears around the corner and he has a bowl of soup in one hand and his phone in the other. His eyes are on the screen, already busy typing up a text as he brings me the soup.

"On it. He was actually just texting me to check on you. I told him I'm pretty sure you have ebola and I'm not bothering to take you to the ER, just tossing you in the basement to decompose with the other skeletons down there. He said that was cool, just squeeze you into a corner since it's cramped."

I roll my eyes, taking the bowl from him. "You're ridiculous." He just smirks, pocketing his phone. He looks more tired than usual and seems less himself. His playfulness seems more forced.

"Everything okay?" I ask, sipping the soup from the spoon. It's hot as fuck but I can tell it's just what my stomach needs. If I can keep it down.

He crosses one arm over his chest and scrubs a hand over the scruff on his face. "Yeah. Just tired."

A wave of dizziness hits me out of nowhere and I shake my head to try and refocus my vision. The outline of him is blurry. I've never passed out before, but it feels like that might be what's about to happen. I open my mouth to speak, and something comes out, but it's not exactly the words my brain is trying to piece together.

"I've been up for literal *days*." He takes a step closer to me and takes the bowl and spoon from my hand, placing it on the end table. "Watching these fucking cameras I lied about not having access to, waiting for you to pull out the wine I sent with Ezra. I *really* wanted the blame for that to be placed on Kruz since it seemed like she was the one who left it here. It would have been *so* much easier for me to take what I needed from your cooling corpse, but here we are." He's so nonchalant, but his words are only slightly registering in my brain because *what the fuck?*

He shoves his hands in his pockets and my head tips back against the couch cushion. I've lost all control of my movements and panic swirls inside me as everything goes dark.

"Just my luck that you'd take one diluted sip of it and puke your guts out immediately after."

29

HE'S A DIPSHIT

JACK

THE DRIVE to the hospital took longer than it should have —closer to four hours, not the three I'd expected. Every minute felt stretched thin by worry. The text that came in this morning from the hospital about Anna's overdose played over and over in my head like a broken record. I wasn't even sure what I'd find when I got here, but I had to come.

Leaving Sienna with Mom was a relief, but it didn't make it easier to leave Quinn behind, especially since she's still sick.

I want to call and check on her one last time before I head inside, but when I do it goes straight to voicemail.

It's been a few hours since I talked with her, and I have assumed she's been sleeping off her sickness. I suppose now she's let her phone die, but that doesn't stop the anxiety that spikes at not being able to hear her voice with everything else that's been going on.

Now that I'm not driving, I pull up the house cameras just to have a peek, like some lovesick stalker.

My system is down, and panic swirls in my gut.

I text Stu to ask if maybe he could go over and check on her, but after a few minutes, I realize he's leaving me on read. He's so fucking unreliable at times and probably ignoring me to just get out of making the trip over.

I dial Ezra, which I should have done in the first place, and he answers after the first ring.

"Jack. What's up?" He sounds like he's saying the words around a mouthful of food.

"Hey, are you busy?" I ask.

He must sense the anxiety in my tone. "Is it Anna?"

"No. Well. I'm not sure, honestly, but that's not why I am calling." I explain the situation with Quinn and ask if he can just pop in really fast to check on her. I had food delivered earlier, but I also ask him to take some ginger ale or something just in case she's sick of drinking Gatorade.

If she's been able to keep anything down at all.

I eye the front of the hospital, regretting leaving her alone now, even for my sister. Maybe it would have been the rude wake up call she needed if I refused to come to her.

I realize I may be overreacting, but Ezra doesn't seem to mind. I guess with everything else that's been going on, my excessive worry is not completely unfounded.

"Oh, yeah. Sure thing," he says, then chugs his drink in my ear.

"I appreciate you. I texted Stu first but he totally blew me off."

"He's a dipshit," he replies. I can hear him rustling around. "I'll go on over now and call you as soon as I'm with her, but I'm sure everything is fine. Don't stress."

I breathe out a sigh of relief, hang up the phone, and drag myself out of the car.

Walking through the sliding doors of the hospital, my heart races. The front desk feels like a barrier between me and the answers I need. I step up to it, trying to keep my voice steady.

"Hi, I'm looking for my sister, Anna Hollis—she was brought in this morning after an overdose."

The receptionist, a woman in her forties, gives me a brief, polite smile before typing on her keyboard. She frowns slightly as she scans the screen, then looks up at me. "I'm sorry, but we don't have anyone by that name admitted here."

I blink, sure I misheard her. "No, there must be a mistake. I got a text from this hospital saying she overdosed and was brought in earlier today."

Her expression softens, but the confusion in her eyes remains. "I understand, but she's not in our system. Let me check again."

I stand there, heart pounding, as she taps a few more keys, scrolling through something I can't see. The moments stretch on painfully until she shakes her head. "I'm really sorry, but there's no record of anyone by that name being treated or admitted here today."

I feel like I've been hit in the chest. The ground feels unsteady beneath me as I struggle to comprehend what she's saying. "So... she was never here?"

The receptionist gives me an apologetic look. "It seems that way. We don't have any record of her."

I'm at a loss. The text—it wasn't a mistake. I know it came

from the hospital. Did someone give me the wrong information? Was it some kind of cruel prank?

I step away from the desk, the receptionist's voice fading as she says something else I barely hear. I pull out my phone, checking the message again. The hospital's number is right there. It's real, but it doesn't make sense.

I dial the number from the message. The line rings twice before a voice answers. "St. Anthony's Hospital, how can I help you?"

"Hi, I got a text this morning saying my sister—Anna Hollis—overdosed and was brought in. I'm at the hospital now, but there's no record of her being here." My voice is tight, barely holding together. "I just needed to check the number the text came from."

There's a pause, followed by some typing. "I'm sorry, but I don't have any record of an Anna being admitted today. Are you sure it was this hospital?"

I clench my teeth, trying to stay calm. "Yes, I'm sure. The message came from this number."

Another pause. "I'm really sorry, sir. I don't know what happened, but there's no information here about your sister. Not to mention that the hospital wouldn't send a *text* about something like this."

I hang up, the weight of confusion and frustration pressing down on me. She was never here. My stomach churns as I stand there in the middle of the hospital, feeling like an idiot. What the hell is going on?

I glance down at my phone, hoping for some kind of response from Quinn or Ezra, but there's still nothing.

30

I'VE NEVER WISHED MORE THAT I COULD PUKE ON SOMEONE

QUINN

I WAKE minutes or maybe hours later, confused.

At first, I think I'm in the dim light of my dorm room, but the last several days come flooding back to me and the hot, sticky liquid running down my arm and dripping off the ends of my fingertips tells me that wherever I am, the scenario is not a good one.

I can hear Kronk barking, losing his fucking mind somewhere in the distance. I must still be at Jack's. A wave of relief washes over me knowing that he is safe.

Or at least seems to be.

"You should be glad I took it out while you were still unconscious." The blurry form of Stu comes into view. He's standing directly in front of me, and I can barely make out his features. Apparently whatever he drugged me with was some strong shit. "I think I would've liked watching you squirm under my knife."

My mouth is dry and my tongue feels heavy. Use of my limbs is out of the question. I can barely hold my head up.

I genuinely have no idea what the fuck he's talking about, and even if I were completely cognizant I am fairly certain I still wouldn't.

My brain wants to be shocked that it's Stu who's doing this to me, wants to be overwhelmed by what is happening, but the drugs in my system aren't allowing room for things like reactions or feelings.

"This was really no trouble at all." He's rolling something around between his fingers, holding it up in front of his face like he's squinting at it. "I just don't know what to do with you in the aftermath since I *planned* for you to be dead for this."

I shift my head against the stone wall, grunting. It's cold wherever we are.

"I could just kill you but I'm not used to getting my hands dirty." He shoves whatever he was looking at in his pocket. "This is a first for me, but I guess there's a first time for everything."

He's pacing now.

I need to buy time. Someone has to come. Maybe Jack will realize something's wrong when I don't answer the phone? I just need to keep Stu talking, and gather information—anything that might give me a chance.

"What... what is that?" My words are almost too quiet, but they seem to reach him. "What did you take from me?"

His smirk widens as he crouches down. "A chip. Your dad had it implanted in you. Didn't know that, did you?" He leans in closer, eyes gleaming with sick satisfaction. "He used it to store information on The Assembly over the years, all the little secrets tucked inside your arm. But don't worry, you're free of that now. Too bad it doesn't free you from me." The smile on his face is tilted and feral. "I usually have someone else do the dirty work for me. Like when I paid those little shits to stomp your dad's head in. Or when I paid Jack's sister to keep him busy for the day, making sure she won't be answering any of his calls once he realizes she's not actually in the hospital. It's crazy what people will do for a little cash, especially when they're hard up for drugs. But here I am, and I can't say I'm not enjoying myself."

Whatever this villain monologue is, I can't take much more of it. I feel like I'm about to pass out again. But those feelings I said I couldn't feel before? I feel them now; so fucking sad for Jack and Sienna.

I hope his sister is at least safe, regardless of how shit a person she is.

My head lolls to the side, my brain finished now that it's thought some thoughts.

Stu crouches in front of me, pricking under my chin with the tip of a fucking 8-inch hunting knife as he tilts my head back upright. The adrenaline rush from him breaking my skin again makes me a little more lucid.

"I know you hated your dad. I hated him too, so we have that in common." His hot breath fans across my face. I've never wished more that I could puke on someone. I'm sure if I try hard enough I can bring that fucking soup back up. "At least, after he tried to step down. Because of course that fucking left me with *this* job. Getting rid of him and getting rid of all the information he had that he could hold over The Assembly that would allow him to walk away from our little *boys' club* unscathed."

I finally find it within myself to form more words. "I don't have any information." They come out slurred, barely audible, and even though I'm speaking, it feels like someone else's voice.

Stu scoffs, amusement flickering in his eyes. "Yeah, not anymore. I just cut the chip out of your arm." He gestures toward my arm, and I glance down, seeing the blood still seeping from the wound. I don't understand how any of this is even possible until I realize the spot he's cut it from is one that already had a scar there.

Suddenly, it all clicks into place. The surgery I had as a child, the sharp pains at the site of the scar, the meetings with my dad, and the way he always gripped me by the arm or shoulder. He wasn't just controlling me emotionally—he was using me to store his secrets, hiding them inside me.

Stu continues, leaning in closer, his voice dripping with condescension. "Your dad thought he could keep secrets from us, that we wouldn't know what he was up to behind closed doors. Guess he didn't realize how closely we were watching. Pretty fucking stupid of him to presume that."

He digs the knife further into my chin and I wince, but I suspect the drugs dull the pain because he seems frustrated that I'm not screaming.

Blood drips down the knife and along his hand and forearms.

I attempt to move my legs, testing if any strength has returned. My toes twitch, and I feel a spark of hope. If I can just distract him enough, maybe I can kick the stack of boxes piled next to me over, and make enough noise to make him falter. I'm grasping at straws, but I feel helpless and hopeless.

"The people we had watching him just moved to you once he was out of the picture."

At least now I know I wasn't actually losing my fucking mind in the weeks leading up to moving in with Jack and Sienna, but I guess my moving in here played right into his plans.

I am thankful that this psychopath opted to get me alone rather than drag the two of them into this mess. I am so glad they're safe and Jack is far, far away.

Though I am not sure I would mind a little help right now.

I was stupid for not realizing he'd drag me into his shady life even though I fought against it every step of the way. I should have known he'd find a way to use me regardless.

I jerk my head back and I feel the tip of the knife release from my skin.

Blood gushes and Stu's entire body shudders.

It's in this moment I realize that he is enjoying this game a little too much, and I am well and truly fucked because I can barely control the muscles in my neck let alone any other part of my body.

"I could do all the things I really want to with you, and hide your body in a place no one will ever find it." He brushes my hair from my face reverently and bile rises in my throat. "Or maybe I'll just leave you here and find a way to frame Jacky Boy for all the depraved shit I'm about to do to you. This is his basement, after all." The smile on his face tells me exactly how he feels about this *depravity*.

The door at the top of the stairs creaks and he jerks

upright but doesn't make it a full step away from me before a shot rings out.

The bullet hits him square in the back and he crumples to the floor in front of me, completely limp as blood pours from the gunshot wound and pools around his lifeless body.

Footsteps pound down the stairs and Ezra comes into view for a split second before I lose consciousness again.

31

CARVED HIM UP LIKE A FUCKING JACK-O-LANTERN

QUINN

MY BODY IS WRACKED with spasms and my mind is spinning in a foggy haze as I struggle to find rest. Every muscle aches and twitches, fighting against whatever foreign substance is coursing through my veins. In the moments when my consciousness flickers back, I hear Jack's voice nearby, his words soothing and reassuring.

His hand is a constant weight on mine, grounding me in the present and reminding me that I am safe now. I try to respond to his whispered words of comfort, but my body is unresponsive and heavy with exhaustion. His touch is the tether that keeps me from drifting too far away.

LATER, when my mind finally clears enough for me to wake and speak, two police officers come into the room to take my statement. Jack's by my side, and their questions blur together, but I answer them as best as I can, even though my body still feels like it's been pulled through hell.

As they're wrapping things up, I glance at my arm, still bandaged where Stu cut the chip out of me. My stomach twists with unease, and I clear my throat. "Do you know what the chip was? The one he took out of my arm?"

The cops exchange a quick glance, one that makes my pulse quicken. A tall, burly officer with a furrowed brow tilts his head slightly. "Chip? Ma'am, we don't have any information about a chip."

My chest tightens. I'm suddenly more alert than I've been since I got here. "Stu... he said he cut it out. That it was storing information, something my dad put there."

The officer who had spoken before shifts uncomfortably, glancing at his partner—a woman with short-cropped hair who's watching me a little too closely, her expression unreadable. "We weren't told anything about that," she says, her voice cool and steady. "If something like that exists, it's not in our report."

The way she says it sets off alarm bells. The tension between them, the quick glances—they're hiding something.

I push myself to sit up slightly, my body protesting with every movement. Jack notices and places a steadying hand on my shoulder, but I can't stop. "You didn't find anything? No sign of the chip at all?" I press, my voice trembling slightly. I can feel my heart pounding in my chest.

The officer shakes her head again, almost too quickly. "No, ma'am. All we've got is evidence from the crime scene, and nothing like that came up." She is adamant.

I narrow my eyes, studying her. There's something off

about their lack of concern and their overly neutral expressions—it feels rehearsed. I catch the slight shift in the male officer's posture like he might try to keep this conversation from going any further.

Jack squeezes my hand, but his touch doesn't ground me this time. Instead, I'm overwhelmed with disappointment. I know I should care more about uncovering whatever The Assembly is hiding, but right now, I just want to be free of it all. I take a deep breath, shaking my head slightly. "I must be imagining things," I say, forcing a weak smile. "Maybe the drugs are messing with my head."

The officers exchange a glance, their expressions shifting to one of relief. "It happens," the female officer says, her tone almost soothing. "You've been through a lot."

I nod, letting the moment pass without pressing further. "Right, of course," I murmur, allowing the suspicion in my voice to fade. I don't want them to see me as anything but a confused patient—or at least, that's how I want them to think I see myself right now.

I don't believe them. Not for a second.

But I have to consider Sienna. I can't go running around playing detective, putting myself in danger, and in turn, my sweet baby and her dad.

As they leave, I watch them go, my suspicion hardening into certainty. The Assembly has its claws in this town, and the cops? They're part of it. But I can't bring myself to dig deeper into it. I'm just relieved to be away from all of that chaos now, which may make me a terrible person but I am not in any place to take them on.

Jack leans in, brushing a reassuring kiss against my forehead.

But as I close my eyes, unease swirls in my gut. I don't trust the police. Still, a part of me is thankful to be removed from the situation. I hope to go on with my life without thinking about any of this again.

JACK

My feet carry me back and forth across the sterile hospital room, my gaze never straying from Quinn's pale form. She looks so fragile lying there, an IV drip attached to her arm and tubes snaking out from beneath her thin hospital gown. Her breathing is shallow but steady, and I can't bear the sight of her in this state.

The rage simmering just beneath my worry threatens to consume me. Suddenly, the door opens and a doctor enters the room, her face etched with a somber expression. My eyes lock with hers as I turn to face her, desperate for any news about what the hell Stu dosed her with. I am thankful she's been awake enough to talk and eat, but it hasn't lessened my worry. She's still sleeping a lot. Too much.

I am still reeling in shock at the thought of someone intentionally hurting her like this, especially one of my best friends—least of all, Stu.

She gets straight to the point, her voice grave and serious. "After thorough testing, we have identified the substance that she ingested. It was a high dose of strychnine, an incredibly toxic poison with potential for severe and life-threatening consequences."

My jaw tightens.

"Luckily, it seems she only consumed a small amount. At higher doses, it can be lethal, but in this case, it was barely enough to cause a severe reaction."

Her words carry a heaviness that lingers in the space between us as I try to process the gravity of the situation. My mind races with thoughts of how easily things could have turned out much worse.

If my *best friend* wasn't already dead I'd have gladly shot him myself. Or strangled him to death. Carved him up like a fucking jack-o-lantern. That probably would have been more satisfying. "What does the recovery for something like this look like?" I ask.

"She will be fine within the next day or so," the doctor says reassuringly. "She's past the worst of it. With some rest and proper care, she should make a quick recovery."

I let out a breath.

She nods and leaves the room, leaving me alone with Quinn again. I climb into bed with her, curling my body around hers as she sleeps fitfully, my mind racing and my heart in fucking pieces.

LATER, I step into the hallway to call Ezra. It rings once before he picks up.

"Jack, how is she?" His voice is filled with concern.

"She's stable," I say, my voice tight.

When he stopped by my house and found a fucking gun lying on the kitchen island—something we both know I do not own—and the door to the basement cracked open, he didn't hesitate to do what needed to be done. He hadn't even realized it was Stu before he pulled the trigger, which is something I am sure will take him a long time to recover from.

The gratitude I feel for this man is immeasurable. Not just for his quick thinking, but because he's caring for Sienna today to give my mom a break and so I can be here with Quinn around the clock.

She babbles in the background and a smile tugs at the corner of my mouth. Smiling is hard right now.

Remaining upright is hard right now.

I'm exhausted and my face is numb from lack of sleep.

"Baby girl has been an angel," he says. "The crazy mutt too."

"Thank you," I say seriously. "For everything."

He is silent for a moment. He's been adamant that he's no hero, that he only did what anyone would have done in such a dire situation. "I'm here for you, man." No truer words have ever been spoken. "Take care of your girl and don't worry about us."

If there's one thing I'm *not* worried about, it's Sienna's safety while she's with Ezra. "Thanks. Give me a call if there's anything you need." My words are loaded, because I don't mean just for Sienna. Processing all that's happened is going to be a trip for all of us.

I end the call and return to Quinn's bedside, my heart heavy. I gently stroke her hair, watching her sleep.

No one will hurt her again, because she's never leaving my fucking sight after this.

32

EVERY PART OF HER IS MINE

JACK

MY HAND SHAKES SLIGHTLY as I insert the key into the lock and turn it. The lock clicks open, and I push the heavy oak door inward, gesturing for Quinn to enter first. As soon as we step inside, the familiar scent of home envelops me, and a wave of relief washes over me unexpectedly. However, my mind is still reeling from the traumatic events of the past few days. I glance at Quinn, her face worn and tired but determined, and worry lays heavy on my shoulders —uncertainty about how Quinn will feel coming home to the place where she experienced something so traumatic.

With the exception of Sienna, there is no comparison to the depth of love I feel for her, surpassing any other person or thing in my life.

Sienna is fast asleep in my arms and I head toward her room to tuck her in for the night.

"I want to hold her." Quinn's voice is tinged with guilt. The thing that amplifies every feeling I have for her most is that she loves my daughter just as much as I do. "I feel so bad that her schedule has been messed up, and she's been away from you so much because of me."

Of course, that's what she's focused on. I shake my head, wrapping my free arm around her. "Sienna and Grammy have loved spending extra time together, and she and Uncle Ezra had a blast. She's fine, Quinn. Let her sleep."

She bites her lip, uncertain, before finally nodding. Her shoulders are tense as she follows me through to the living room and sinks into the couch. I take Sienna upstairs, and when I return I take a moment to properly look at my love. Her face is pale, her eyes tired, but she is here.

She is safe.

"I was so fucking scared," I admit, my voice breaking slightly. I sit beside her, pulling her body into mine.

As she leans into me, tears stream down her cheeks, leaving a trail of glistening tracks. I can feel the weight of her pent-up emotions as she finally lets go and allows herself to cry in my arms.

For several minutes, she clings to me, her body shaking with sobs as her tears soak into my shirt. As I hold her tightly, the heaviness of my own pain from this entire situation presses down on me. It's nearly unbearable at times, but especially seeing her like this.

It's not that I mourn the loss of my best friend; in reality, he was never who I thought he was and his end was deserved. What hurts me is the realization that Quinn has endured so much in her life, only to have it all culminate to this. I did everything I could to protect her and do the right thing, but I couldn't stop this from happening. And now we both have to deal with the outcome.

When her breathing finally steadies, she sits up and wipes her tear-streaked cheeks with the sleeve of her shirt. "I love you," I whisper, brushing away the remaining tears with my thumb. My large hand cups her face as she kisses me softly, her lips still damp from crying. We are both tentative at first, but our longing for each other quickly takes over.

I have missed her so much; I need to be as close to her as humanly possible, need to feel she's safe. She slept nearly constantly while she was in the hospital—which was needed for her recovery and I was thankful to just be there with her— but I wanted my best friend back through every second of it. And while I need to be gentle with her, I can't control the need I feel to be inside her right fucking now.

I slowly undress her, my hands gentle and cautious as they glide over her wounded body. A surge of anger pulsates through me as I get a closer look at her injuries, her skin a mosaic of deep cuts and dark bruises. It breaks my heart to see her hurt in this way, but there is also a twisted part of me that is furious that Stu was the one to leave these marks on her skin when it should have been me.

Every part of her is *mine*.

She belongs to me, and her body is *mine to mark*.

She deserves scars that remind her she is loved and adored, not ones that hold the memories they do, and I have every intention of changing that for her if and when she's ready and willing to let me.

"I love you." Her warm lips press against mine again as I gently guide her naked body onto the couch, determined to worship every inch of her.

My fingertips dance lightly over her taut skin, tracing

every curve and dip with the urge I have to break it barely in check. The softness of her flesh sparks a flame inside me.

My mouth travels down her neck, over her breasts, and along her stomach, until I reach my destination between her legs.

I gently spread her lips with my tongue, her pretty pink pussy already glistening with her own juices. "Mmm," I moan against her clit, hoping the vibration sets her on edge a little. I want to erase every thought from her mind. "You missed me too."

She covers her eyes with her forearm, her muscles tensing as I push her closer to the brink. Then she lets go, trembling in waves as I lick her through it.

"Was that too much?" I ask the question in between kisses as I work my way back up her body.

"Not enough." She locks her legs around my waist and pulls me against her core. I'm still dressed, but that's a quick fix.

"I don't want to hurt you," I tell her, simultaneously whipping my shirt off and unbuttoning my pants.

"I don't mind the pain if it's coming from you."

I pause my movements and release a whispered *fuck*.

She has no idea what she's asking for.

I push myself inside of her, and she tightens around me. As I do, she asks, "Do you get off on the thought of me getting pleasure from the pain you cause?" The way her pussy is squeezing my cock tells me she gets off on it a little too.

"No." I pump into her slowly. "The thought of carving my name into your skin does it for me, though," I admit, and the look on her face spurs me on. I decide to test the waters even further. There's nothing wrong with fantasizing even if she doesn't actually want to act on it later.

I run my fingers over the cut near her shoulder. It's deep, and it will scar something awful, unlike the laceration under her chin that didn't even require a stitch. "Once you're all healed up, can I break this skin again? Replace the scar with one of my own?"

She nods fervently and pulls my lips against hers, seemingly embarrassed to admit that she'd like that as much as I would.

We both need therapy, but in the meantime, I plan to fuck the ghosts from her head.

My body moves in a primal rhythm, thrusting into her with urgency and need. My fingers dance over her swollen clit, bringing her to the brink of pleasure again. The sound of our skin slapping together echoes through the room and I am consumed by the desire to fill her up, my movements becoming more urgent and intense. Nothing else exists except for the raw, carnal connection between us and the unexplainable love we feel for each other.

She gasps and arches her back, her nails digging into my skin, as I give her every inch of me over and over with relentless intensity.

With one final thrust, I groan as I spill into her, her tight pussy squeezing every last drop from my body as she shudders beneath me.

Our hearts pound in sync, our souls fusing together in the aftermath.

We lay tangled up, catching our breath and grateful to be together again. In this moment, I am overflowing with a peaceful certainty that everything will be okay, and our love for one another will only continue to grow and flourish beyond this single moment together. We will recover, and I am determined to do whatever it takes to walk with her through this process and make sure she emerges stronger than before.

33

SPOILER ALERT: WHAT I NEED IS ALWAYS HIM

QUINN

AS THE CITY street blurs into a long, winding road, my thoughts drift back to the first time I drove to Jack's house. It feels like a lifetime ago.

This time, I'm not alone.

So much has happened in such a short period. When I initially came to him and Sienna, I simply wanted to make it through until I arrived at the next thing in my life.

I gained so much more than I bargained for.

Despite all the trauma I've faced, I find myself feeling oddly at ease. Tears have been shed, and for someone who rarely cries, it's been a lot. But Jack has been there with me through it all; he's cried too. Even though I received the brunt of all that happened, he also experienced significant loss in the process.

I can't imagine losing my best friend in this way, and while he wasn't who Jack thought he was, that doesn't make it any less devastating. Thankfully, he and Ezra are above any kind of toxic masculinity bullshit, and they have leaned on each other a lot. I am thankful they have each other.

And poor Ezra... I literally cannot comprehend what he must be feeling. I am so fucking lucky that he came over when he did, and I am pretty sure I'll spend every day for the rest of my life telling him how grateful I am that he didn't hesitate when he realized what was happening.

Now, as Jack squeezes my thigh when we turn onto his long driveway, I'm brought back to the present. He puts the car into park and walks around the front before coming over to my side and opening the door for me.

Such a gentleman; unlike Kronk, who I can already hear going nuts in the backyard.

When I get out of the car, Jack wraps me in a bear hug, and I nuzzle into his chest, breathing in his bergamot scent. Tears form in my eyes because at one point, just a few short days ago, I thought I'd never smell him again.

Never feel this again.

His arms tighten around me as if he can sense my thoughts, pulling me closer until there's no space left between us.

We stand like that for some time before he kisses me on the forehead and pulls away from me. He opens the back car door and unbuckles Sienna, cradling her gently in his arms. The three of us head inside, and as we step through the door, I hear familiar voices coming from the living room.

"Hey, we're back!" I call out, my voice echoing through the space.

Kruz and Ezra are already here, having arrived just before us. They let themselves in, per usual, as they're here more often than not lately. Kruz has been constantly at my side, acting like a mother hen even though I have been mostly fine since returning home from the hospital.

She stands up from the couch and walks over, her face softening when she sees Sienna in Jack's arms. "There's the little princess," she says, reaching out to take Sienna, who goes willingly into her arms.

She never really warmed up to Ezra before, but seems surprisingly at ease around him now. As I watch them, I notice how her usual guardedness has softened; she's more relaxed, more herself. She recognizes that Ezra's been through his own kind of hell too, a hell maybe worse than what Jack and I have endured. She's grateful to him for saving her best friend, and that gratitude is starting to break down the walls she had up around him.

Ezra joins them, a small smile tugging at the corner of his lips as Kruz hands Sienna to him. He's gentle with her, holding her like she's something precious. There's a moment when Kruz and Ezra are talking, and I hear Kruz laugh—a real laugh, the kind I haven't heard from her in literal *days* because of how anxious she's been about my wellbeing in the aftermath of all this.

Seeing them together, laughing, even if just for a moment, makes me realize how much he might actually need someone like her in his life. Kruz is a light and her friendship is a joy. Maybe, in some way, she could help him heal a little.

I know having her around helps me.

Jack and I watch from the doorway as Ezra and Kruz move to the back patio, Sienna nestled in Ezra's arms. Jack slips his hand into mine, squeezing gently as we follow them outside. The late afternoon sun casts a warm glow over every-thing, and for a moment, it feels like the world has stopped spinning so fast.

Ezra and Jack settle into their usual spots on the patio, beers now in hand, talking in low voices. Kruz sits close to Ezra, her laughter occasionally drifting across the space as she plays with Sienna's tiny hands. I lean against the door-frame, my heart swelling with a mixture of gratitude and something deeper, something I wasn't sure I was ready to accept yet.

Something that feels like a real family.

But it's there, undeniable, like a warmth spreading through my chest.

As I watch them, I feel a sense of peace, a rare moment of calm in the storm that has been our lives lately. Whatever comes next, I know we'll face it together—this little makeshift family of ours, finding solace in each other's company.

Jack must sense the same thing because he walks over to me, his presence steady and grounding like he knows exactly what I need without me having to say a word.

Spoiler alert: what I need is *always* him.

We stand there for a moment, wrapped up in each other, letting the world fade away. Eventually, he pulls back just enough to look down at me, his eyes soft and full of some-thing that feels like home, like safety.

"I love you," he says softly, though we've said it many times before now, it feels new every time.

"I love you too, Jack," I reply, the words as natural as breathing.

And as our lips meet in a gentle, lingering kiss.

"Get a room," Ezra chides, and when I look his way he's covering Sienna's eyes with his hand and grinning from ear to ear.

As the sun dips below the horizon, casting long shadows across the porch, I realize that even when everything goes sideways, there are moments like this—moments where things feel almost normal. It's weird how life keeps going, how you can still laugh and find comfort with the people who matter, even after everything. Maybe that's what gets us through—the little bits of normalcy we hold on to, even when everything else feels like it's falling apart. And as we all sit here, talking quietly while Sienna makes those cute baby noises, I can't help but think that, somehow, we're all going to be okay.

I look up at Jack again.

Better than okay.

Amongst all the noise in my mind lately, there's been one constant, a whisper that's always there, even on the hardest days. Sometimes it's soft, other times it's more like a whisper *shout*, but it's the one I trust most. The one that tells me, without a doubt, that Jack and Sienna are my forever.

34

THE BEGINNING

EZRA

THE QUIET OF the night is interrupted by the sound of a car pulling up outside my house. I glance at the clock—3:00 a.m. I am instantly alert, moving silently to the window to see who has arrived. When I recognize the blacked out Sedan, a mix of annoyance and relief surges through me.

Slipping on a jacket, I step outside, closing the door quietly behind me. My former best friend is waiting by the car, his face illuminated by the dim streetlight.

He looks tired.

Fuck him.

He takes a deep breath, his expression grim. "I've taken care of everything. I've anonymously submitted a shit ton of evidence to the police. Stu is well on his way to being the scapegoat for everything; stalking, manipulation, Marshall's murder, and various other crimes tied to The Assembly. You're in the clear, and I'm still as good as dead."

I study his face for any sign of deceit. "You're sure?"

Stu shakes his head. "I made sure everything was airtight. I couldn't live with myself if I didn't set things straight. It's all there—documents, recordings, every bit of evidence that links me to our crimes, and nothing that implicates anyone else. The Assembly remains a ghost."

I stare at him, violent anger simmering beneath my calm exterior.

Stu was my best friend, but that didn't stop him from being a complete psycho. The way he went after Jack's girl was beyond anything I can forgive, and I don't feel guilty for shooting him, or for the fact that I'll likely never see him again after tonight.

He was supposed to retrieve the chip her father implanted in her, the one holding all the information Marshall had over the Assembly's head keeping him immune from the consequences of attempting to step down from his position.

As Stu talks, I slip a hand into my pocket, fingers brushing against the small metal chip now in my possession. I feel the ridges of it beneath my fingertips, its weight surprisingly significant for something so small. The chip that holds the secrets her father thought would save him—secrets that could destroy the Assembly if they ever saw the light of day.

But they won't. Not if I have anything to say about it.

I don't give a fuck about the rest of The Assembly, but I do give a fuck about the things on there that could implicate *me*.

And there's plenty.

There were simpler solutions, and ways to get the job

done without causing her harm. But Stu? He couldn't resist taking it too far, hurting her in the process, all because he got off on pushing boundaries and playing god.

I should have known better than to trust him with something so important, but it is what it is.

I've always done everything I can to make sure Jack and his family stay out of this. I've kept him in the dark for years, and I'll keep doing it. Just because *I'm* stuck with The Assembly doesn't mean he has to be involved.

Sure, the things I've kept from him became overly complicated when he got involved with Quinn, but we're past that being an issue.

"Don't think this absolves you for being so fucking messy." Stu is fucking stupid, unhinged, and the way he has always idolized all The Assembly stands for has clouded his judgment more than once. "You need to disappear, and not just from Hallow Ridge. I don't care if I ever fucking hear from you again. You'll be a lot better off if I *don't.*"

Without another word, he nods and turns and gets back into his car, driving off into the night. I watch him go.

I return inside, closing the door quietly behind me. As I make my way back to the bedroom, I pause and pull out my phone to respond to the text Jack sent inviting me to go golfing this weekend.

Sliding back into bed beside Kruz, I feel her stir slightly, her hand reaching for me.

She mumbles something in her sleep, leaning into me. I lay awake for a long time, knowing that when I fall asleep, she'll be gone by the time I wake again.

But that's fine.

She won't get far.

Because of all the plans I've had in my life, the ones I have to keep her coming back are by far the best.

EPILOGUE
QUINN

6 MONTHS LATER...

EARLIER TONIGHT, I stood at my graduation, a moment I hadn't thought possible just half a year ago, or even *three* months ago when my mom passed away and I had to overcome that hurdle as well.

The auditorium buzzed with the low hum of families and friends, but my mind kept drifting back to everything I had overcome just to make it there. From the stage, I watched Jack in the crowd, Sienna perched on his lap, her tiny hands clapping along with the audience.

She's grown so much over the past six months, and watching her meet each milestone along the way has been nothing short of amazing.

Ezra sat beside them, and Kruz's bright smile from a few rows over from me was the same steady source of warmth I had come to depend on.

When I crossed the stage, pride swelled in my chest. The cap on my head somehow made me feel lighter than the burdens I'd carried through the years, and the diploma in my hands wasn't just a certificate—it was proof of everything I'd fought through. The applause echoed in my ears, but it was Jack's smile that made me feel the most proud. I couldn't help but think of all the nights he had stayed up with me, encouraging me to keep going when I wanted to give up.

After the ceremony, we all gathered outside in the cool evening air. Sienna tugged at my gown, giggling, and I bent down to scoop her up, her joy contagious as I smothered her fat cheeks in kisses.

I often think of all the things Anna is missing out on with her daughter, but I'm eternally grateful to have this place in Sienna's life. Jack cut his sister off after learning she had been involved in Stu's fucked up little game, and he's made it clear he has no plans to forgive her—whether she knew the full extent of what was happening at the time or not. But she hasn't tried to reach out anyway.

For the first time in what felt like forever, I realized the future was mine to shape. Standing there, surrounded by the people I loved—people who had been with me through the worst—I knew I wasn't just celebrating my graduation. I was celebrating survival.

Jack's house is dark and silent, Sienna having gone for a sleepover with Uncle Ezra for the night—and Kronk as well because they both insisted. I never imagined my *dog* having sleepovers for funsies, but here we are.

Kruz volunteered to help babysit after a celebratory

dinner at our favorite restaurant—not that Ezra needs help. He's great with Sienna, and I'm sure there are a million other things Kruz could have chosen to do on her graduation night. More and more every day I wonder when she will finally admit to herself that Ezra is more than just a fling to her.

The way he looks at her, she's definitely more than just a fling to him.

I unstrap my heels as soon as we walk through the front door, anxious to get the death traps off my feet.

I wrap my free hand around Jack's forearm to steady myself, and the way he looks at me tells me he has no intentions of us making it to the bedroom before *our* celebration begins.

I kick my shoes to the side and turn my body toward his, reaching up to clasp my hands around the back of his neck as he closes and locks the front door behind him.

I pull him down for a kiss, and he releases me to turn and set the alarm—some things are non-negotiable after everything we've been through. I appreciate that he always puts our safety first, even though there's not much to worry about these days.

I don't have time to react when he spins back toward me, pulling me against him and pinning my wrists behind my back with his large hand. He assaults me with kisses, and I'm completely lost to him.

Putty.

Goo.

He can do whatever he wants with me.

"You're so easy to make submit," he hums against my

neck, kissing me between each word and I already feel drunk and lax.

This man short circuits my brain, and it's hard to find it within myself to want to push back against him when he handles me like this, but he likes it when I do.

"Am I?" I whisper, barely loud enough for him to hear. Then, without warning, I twist out of his grip and dash toward the stairs, laughing as I go.

His startled chuckle follows me, and I can hear the sound of his footsteps as he takes off after me. "Oh, you think you're getting away that easily?" he calls, amusement lacing his voice.

I leap up the first few steps, glancing back with a grin, but I can barely make out the outline of him in the dark.

He closes the distance with ease, but I squeal and dart up two more steps, my heart racing with anticipation.

I hear him right behind me, his footsteps heavy and determined. "You're only making this worse for yourself," he teases, his voice getting closer.

I laugh, trying to speed up, but I know it's only a matter of seconds before he catches me. "*Worse?* Yeah, okay."

As I reach the top of the stairs, his hand catches my waist, and I let out a yelp as he spins me around. "Got you," he says, grinning down at me. Before I can protest, he scoops me up effortlessly, tossing me over his shoulder like I weigh nothing.

I'm laughing uncontrollably now, playfully pounding my fists against his back. "Put me down!"

He gives a mock sigh, carrying me toward our bedroom. "You never learn, do you?"

"You love it," I shoot back, breathless with laughter.

He gives my thigh a gentle squeeze. "Maybe. But now you're at my mercy."

"My favorite place to be," I giggle.

With one arm holding me in place by the back of my knees, he uses his other to undo and remove his belt. I am slightly disappointed that it's dark and I'm hanging upside down because there's nothing hotter than watching Daddy Jack remove his belt one handed.

He plants me on my feet in the hallway next to his bedroom door and presses my back against the cool wall. With a swift movement, he wraps his belt around my wrists, securing them above my head. Trapped between his body and the wall, I feel both vulnerable and exhilarated.

I squirm playfully, mostly because I want him to be a little rougher. "I can get out of this." I can't, and he knows that as well as I do, but I tease him nonetheless.

He reaches into his back pocket and pulls out a knife, flicking it open with ease. The act is far sexier than any sane person would ever consider it.

The glint of the blade catches my eye as he stabs it through his thick leather belt, effortlessly piercing the wall behind me and pinning me in place. "Can you?"

The question now isn't whether I can or not, but whether *I want to.*

And when Jack drops to his knees in front of me, I decide that *no...* I do not.

He pulls another knife out, and Quinn six months ago would have asked, *"What in the literal fuck?"*—but present-day Quinn knows, loves, and accepts her man.

And all of his quirks and stabby little tendencies.

He's marked my body more times than I can count at this point, and I have found that I love it just as much as he does.

His knives have left scars all over my skin, a reminder of our passionate and intense love. The sharp sting against my skin is addicting, making me crave more of his touch. I can't get enough of the pleasure and pain he brings, willingly giving myself over to his skilled hands. With each new mark, our bond seems to grow stronger, and it's something I am not sure either of us will ever get enough of.

He grasps my thigh, his fingers digging into the soft flesh. I flinch as he pierces my skin, but he quickly soothes the sting, leaning in and tracing circles over the spot with his tongue, causing a jolt of pleasure to shoot through me. As he continues this pattern, the mix of pleasure and discomfort sends shivers down my spine.

I don't even try to bite back the moan that slips out.

"God, you're so fucking dirty," He says against my inner thigh, kissing his way toward where I need his mouth most. "You love the pain as much as I love to inflict it."

He bunches the fabric of my skirt and yanks it up to my waist, exposing my hips. He twists the crotch of my panties around his fist, tearing them from my body with a loud rip, the force of it pulling me forward.

My wrists yank free from the wall, the knife clattering to the floor.

I reach down and grip the hair at the nape of his neck tightly, his belt still binding my wrists, and my heart pounding in my chest as the intensity of what I feel for him.

With a flick of his tongue, he traces a wet path across my

lower abdomen and down the crease of my thigh, pausing to suck and nibble at my sensitive spots. He plunges his face between my legs, eagerly lapping up every drop of my arousal as I writhe and moan under him. My body undulates with pleasure as he expertly works me over the edge until I can no longer control the sounds coming from my mouth and the jerky movements I make as I come undone and drench his face.

He lifts me up and wraps my legs tightly around his waist. My back presses against the door, pushing it open as he carries me effortlessly to the bed. With a swift movement, he tosses me onto the soft mattress. As he undoes his pants, I can see the hunger in his eyes. Without hesitation, he settles himself between my thighs and thrusts into me, causing the bed to shake beneath us as he fucks me into the mattress. The sound of our moans fills the room as we lose ourselves in each other.

"*Fuck*. Marry me," he whispers the words against the shell of my ear between rough thrusts.

I probably shouldn't take them as seriously as I do in the throes of passion, but I answer seriously anyway. "Yes," the word comes out a grunt with the way he ruts into me, but he stills when he hears it, fully seated inside me, our pelvises flush with one another.

"*Yes?*" He rests his sweaty forehead against mine.

All I can do is nod and kiss him softly on the lips.

Apparently he likes that because without another movement on either of our parts, his body twitches against mine as he fills me up.

I grin against his mouth because I love that I have this effect on him, and also because...

We are engaged now?

Maybe not... that was probably not for serious.

But then he pulls out of me and shifts his body, taking something from his pocket.

How much shit can those pockets hold?

He unbinds my hands, kissing the tender spots on my wrists from where the leather of his belt had cut into them.

Then, so tenderly, he slips a ring on my finger.

My mouth falls open in shock.

"That wasn't how I planned to ask you, but I planned to ask you nonetheless."

I can't find words.

My eyes fill with tears that immediately spill over my cheeks.

"Say something, baby."

Through bleary eyes, I manage to whisper, "I already said yes, do you want me to say it again?"

His face breaks into a grin as he pulls me closer. "Yes."

"*Yes.*" The weight of the ring on my finger feels both foreign and right, a symbol of the love that binds us together in this moment.

As we hold each other close, I can't help but think back to all the moments that have led us here—the highs and lows, the laughter and tears. It's as if everything has been building up to this one perfect moment, where he asks me to be his forever.

I think I've known he and Sienna would be my forever

from the start. They are the only things that have ever felt sure in my life.

In this embrace, with his heartbeat steady against mine, I know that whatever the future holds, we will face it together. With him by my side, I feel like I can conquer the world. And as we lay here, lost in each other's arms, I know that this is just the beginning of our greatest adventure yet.

ALSO BY GENNA BLACK

Haverhill Burning

Fate Trace Series

No Small Sin

Sinners Keepers

Dead to Sin

Hallow Ridge Series

Whatever Whispers

Whatever Wakes

ACKNOWLEDGMENTS

This book wouldn't be in your hands without the support, love, and feedback from so many people who helped shape it along the way.

First, a massive thank you to Katie. Your endless encouragement, thoughtful insights, and steady presence through this journey have meant the world to me. You've been my sounding board, cheerleader, and co-conspirator, and I honestly couldn't have done it without you. Thank you for believing in this story when I needed it most.

Vanessa, my critique partner extraordinaire—you are a rockstar. From the never-ending support you give me in all things to the detailed feedback that whipped this story into shape, your friendship is invaluable. I'm so grateful to have had you by my side throughout this wild ride, and always.

To my amazing alpha readers, thank you for diving into the messy early drafts with excitement and giving me the confidence to keep going. Your insights, enthusiasm, and love for this story have been incredible motivators. I'm beyond grateful for each of you.

A huge thank you as well to my beta readers—your thoughtful feedback and patience as I tinkered with every detail helped polish this book to where it needed to be. You are all amazing.

My ARC readers, hello and wtf? There were so many of you this time and I am still floored by the response I've gotten on this book. Thank you so much for taking a chance on me and my first dark academia little baby. I appreciate you more than you will ever know!

To Alice, for always being there for me, even when our lives are both absolute chaos. You are a constant source of love and support, and I appreciate you more than words can say.

To Melnard, for keeping me supplied with ginger ale—your contributions toward my sanity may have been our saving grace here.

To my lil Tater Punkin Genevieve, for always believing in me and encouraging me to see the bigger picture and keep going.

To my friends, Ashley, Bea, & all of my TGC & BM besties, thank you for the love and laughter that kept me sane during this process. You're the best kind of people, and I'm lucky to have you in my life.

To my dog Yzma, who inspired the one and only Kronk—thank you for your constant companionship and for being the best muse I didn't know I needed. You've given me more ideas than you'll ever know (and probably more distractions too).

To my PA, Kali, thank you for putting up with me, my chaos, and my never-ending stream of messages. You are an absolute gem, and I couldn't ask for a better partner in crime.

And to my husband, for always being there with your unwavering support, your faith in me and my dreams has kept me going more times than I can count. Thank you for being my anchor.

I love and appreciate all of you so freaking much!

Honorable mentions: Vanessa and Brit for letting me borrow your last names, my ADHD meds, my anxiety meds, my depression meds, Lindslee (you beautiful creature), my sister, Samyang Spicy Chicken Noodle Carbonara Flavor Ramen, 4.58 oz, 5 Pack, Canada Dry Caffeine Free Zero Sugar Ginger Ale Soda Pop, 12 fl oz, 12 Pack Cans, Bert McCracken, all Octavia Jensen books, 59° weather, Taco Bell Nacho Fries, and YOU.

ABOUT THE AUTHOR

Genna Black is a romance author who juggles writing and raising her hell spawn alongside her aggressively supportive husband. Fueled by excessive amounts of caffeine and spicy ramen (and a necessary dose of antidepressants and ADHD medication), she finds great joy in crafting stories that will make you giggle while keeping you on the edge of your seat. With a knack for the steamier side of romance, she hopes to offer readers an escape from the dumpster fire that life can sometimes be.

facebook.com/authorgennablack
instagram.com/authorgennablack
goodreads.com/gennablack
bookbub.com/authors/genna-black

Made in the USA
Las Vegas, NV
06 November 2024

11184638R00173